noticing D
twirling her
the question, "Are you ever going to ask me out on a date?"

The look on his face told her he was as shocked by her query as she was for asking it. He remained silent, his eyes searching hers for answers she didn't have.

She continued, "Ever since we met, I've tried to flirt with you. But you seem to avoid me like the plague. I've come up with several possible reasons for this." Jillian lifted her fingers to count. "Number one, you're already seeing someone—probably that really beautiful girl with the hideous glasses who is always at your side. Number two, you're gay. Or three, you're not interested because I'm not your type."

She stopped and looked at her fingers and then back at him. "Wait, there is a fourth. You're also training to be a priest and have taken an oath of celibacy. That's it, isn't it?"

Leaning close to her, he whispered, "Nope."

She matched his gesture and moving toward him so their noses were almost touching, whispered back, "What is it, then?"

She stared at his slightly-parted lips. Her breathing became shallow and uneven. Before she knew it, he put his hands on the sides of her face and pressed his warm lips, ever so gently, to hers. Every hair on her body tingled, and goose bumps ran down her back.

He pulled away slightly from her, their noses still touching.

Praise for Andrea O'Day

"*LIKE ME OR NOT*, Andrea P. O'Day's novel, captures the ups and downs of Alexis Garett's roller coaster love life with humor and heart. A great give-to-a-girlfriend read!"

~*Kathryn Elliott, author of Adding Lib*
~*~

"Escape into *LIKE ME OR NOT* for a lighthearted romance with a twist in its tail. Again Andrea O'Day shows a particularly skillful use of language to keep the reader engaged. Andrea's unique turn of phrase is sure to produce a smile, or in some cases even a burst of laughter."

~*Anne Ashby, author of Impossible Liaison*
~*~

"Readers who enjoy a witty heroine and want a glimpse of dating disasters will enjoy this book."

~*Renee Ashley Williams, erotic romance author*

To the Ta-Tas

by

Andrea O'Day

This is a work of fiction. Names, characters, places, and incidents are either the product of the author's imagination or are used fictitiously, and any resemblance to actual persons living or dead, business establishments, events, or locales, is entirely coincidental.

To the Ta-Tas

COPYRIGHT © 2016 by Andrea O'Day

All rights reserved. No part of this book may be used or reproduced in any manner whatsoever without written permission of the author or The Wild Rose Press, Inc. except in the case of brief quotations embodied in critical articles or reviews.
Contact Information: info@thewildrosepress.com

Cover Art by *Debbie Taylor*

The Wild Rose Press, Inc.
PO Box 708
Adams Basin, NY 14410-0708
Visit us at www.thewildrosepress.com

Publishing History
First *Last Rose of Summer* Edition, 2016
Print ISBN 978-1-5092-1131-9
Digital ISBN 978-1-5092-1132-6

Published in the United States of America

Dedication

In loving memory to every woman who has
had cancer and beat it,
and to the family and memories of those who didn't,
and to the ones who are conquering it.
Life if too short for regrets
and saying Shoulda, Woulda, Coulda.
And to my editor Maggie Johnson
who could take my words and ideas
and spin her magic to make it sound perfect.
Without you and your guidance,
I wouldn't be successful.
You are the best.

Chapter 1

Current Day

If this was a book, there would be mention of the large school clock on the wall opposite her desk and the sound of the ticking as the hands moved closer to the time she needed to leave. If this was a movie, there would be the shot of rain hitting the window. But this was neither. This was Jillian Taylor's life—her life with the only children she'd ever have, the students at Vickery Elementary School just north of Lexington where she was the principal.

Though aware of the time and the rain, her attention was on the sullen Luke Walton. The shiner covered half his face, and he was hunched over in the chair. The contusion was there that morning when he stepped off the school bus. It was another day with Luke bearing a bruise. Another day in which his teacher would question what happened only to have him shrug his shoulder and mumble that "It's nothing." They never believed him.

Jillian's heart went out to this little boy. Tenderness and sadness appeared in his eyes when he thought no one was looking. Every other time, they were indifferent and hard. But she knew.

She had known someone just like him extremely well decades earlier. It seemed that every few years there would a boy just like Luke sitting in front of her—the stooped shoulders, eyes and ears that had seen and heard too much. It was at these times, she thought of *him* and what he had told her of his stolen childhood.

And for every child like him who sat in her office, she told the same story. *His story.* And then she'd dream about him. She hated waking up the next morning because she never wanted those dreams to end.

She wondered what he was doing. Yet she was a coward. All she had to do was ask Lynda Laughlin the at least twice-a-week school volunteer who recently interviewed for the first-grade teacher position. Lynda's husband, Eric, had been *his* best friend. Though she'd been the principal here for six years, she'd never once seen Eric. However, she knew it was the same Eric Laughlin because the son looked just like his father.

One time, she and Tara drove by Lynda and Eric's house, just to see how he lived. It was ironic how people who were once so close became so distant even when they lived in the same town. Though she had a different last name, she often wondered if *he* knew she was here.

She quickly snapped out of day-dreaming when she heard the rain beat harder on the glass.

"Luke, I'm not going to call your parents," Jillian finally said.

Luke stopped chewing on his lips. His depressed blue eyes looked at her.

"But I am going to talk to Dean about what happened," she said.

Dean's parents were quite sure he was an angel and could do no wrong. Dean was not only sneaky but very manipulative. She dreaded the thought of having to talk to his parents. Again.

"Luke, next time he does that, you go to one of the teachers or you can even ask for me. Do you hear me?"

He nodded. Finally he said, "My dad said I needed to be tougher and fight like a man. He says if I don't stand up for myself, then everyone's just going to keep beating me up."

"Like your dad does?" she asked.

The tear in the nine-year-old's eye rolled down his cheek as he nodded.

"You need to fight with your mind, not your fists. Did I ever tell you about a friend of mine? You remind me so much of him. His dad was just like yours. My friend would hide from him. He would hide at the public library. And when it closed, he'd sneak home after his dad was passed out on the couch. And you know what became of him?"

Luke looked up, his eyes wide as he listened.

"He went to college, on a scholarship, and became a doctor."

"Are you still friends with him?" Luke asked.

She couldn't answer and instead shook her head before continuing, "But there's a lesson here for you. Education and knowledge—your dad can't take those from you. The teachers here can help you, me included." She held out her pinky finger to him. "But for us to help you, you need to pinky-swear not to use your fists. Promise?"

He nodded and linked his small pinky finger in hers. This was Jillian's third child in six years she had pinky-promised with. Her first graduated from high school as valedictorian last year.

There was hope in Luke's blue eyes.

"We're here for you, Luke. But you have to trust us and talk with us."

She glanced at her watch after he nodded. With the rain, she should've left five minutes ago. She was now officially late for her meeting with the school superintendent, yet again.

Unlinking her finger from Luke's, she said, "What we promised stays here. You can't tell anyone but your teachers. And if your dad does this again, you come see me or Ms. Gallagher, the counselor. We'll help you."

He stood. "Thank you Mrs. Taylor."

When he left, she quickly opened her bottom drawer to get her purse while shutting down her computer. Walking out her office, she pulled on her red raincoat.

"Drive carefully," Ellen Davis, her assistant said. "It's raining really hard."

****

The rain matched his mood—gloomy and dark. The dampness caused his hip to ache more. Dr. David Rainier was forty-six, and arthritis was setting in quickly. At this rate, he'd be walking like an old man before he was fifty. It didn't matter that people thought him to be older than he really was. And if anyone asked, he didn't care. He popped a few more ibuprofen to ease the throbbing pain.

The elevator opened to the packed Emergency Room. Leave it to bad weather to fill this place. What was it that Eric liked about working in this part of the hospital? Being the cardiologist on call, once a week, was more than enough for David.

The nurse at the center desk scowled when he approached. Not unexpected, as she wore a perpetual frown.

Before he could ask, she barked, "He's in the doctor's lounge taking a call."

Limping toward the corner room, he opened the door where Eric stood looking out the window, phone to his ear and shaking his head.

"Lynda, I hear what you're saying, but I'm not sure about it. You know firsthand what some of those kids are like, and now you want them in our house?" He paused. "Can we talk about this later when I get home? We're slammed here, and I can't really think about this right now." There was another pause. "Yes, I promise, tonight."

He put the phone in his coat pocket.

"Trouble?" David asked.

Eric Laughlin, his best friend since medical school, spun around, surprised that anyone was there.

"I love my wife, but for the life of me, I'll never understand the way women's brains operate. You know how Lynda has been stir-crazy being a stay-at-home mom since the kids are in school? Well, she interviewed for that open teaching position at the school. And now she tells me that she's been thinking that if she doesn't get this job, she'd like to be a foster mom because then she'd feel like she was helping children. This is from the woman who originally never wanted to be a mother and cried the entire first month we found out she was pregnant with child number one. Now she wants more, twenty-four/seven."

"For your sake, I hope she gets the job." David leaned against the counter. "Glad I never married and had a family."

Eric began to laugh. "If that's what you want to tell

yourself, go ahead. But here is why you're not married…"

"Don't go *there*," David mumbled.

"You are not a happy-go-lucky person, like me. You make everyone around you miserable, or you run them off. And you know what I am talking about. The only person who wants to be with you is Cathy. And she's certainly no ray of sunshine. Speaking of which, what is going on with you two?"

David stared at him. "I have no idea what you're talking about?"

"She's been here, what, a week? And you two were seen at Anthony's having dinner the other night."

"It was just one dinner. It's nothing."

"Well?" Eric asked.

There were times, he thought, *Eric had the gossip gene programmed into this DNA.*

"There's nothing to report. She's looking for a place to be able to settle down, and I reluctantly agreed to dinner."

Eric raised his one eyebrow. "She's *looking* for husband number two. I think we both know who she has in mind for that."

Before David could respond, the nurse from the front desk opened the door.

"Dr. Laughlin, there's been a multiple-car accident. Truck skidded through an intersection. Five victims are coming in now."

Limping, David followed Eric out of the lounge.

An EMT shouted, "Fifty-four, male. Broken leg and contusions to the head."

David continued to limp toward the line of stretchers coming down the hall. At the front of the entrance, Eric and another doctor were quickly evaluating the patients and sending them to the various triage rooms.

Female, age forty-two," the male EMT said loudly, but calmly. He held an oxygen mask over her face. "Was rammed in the side by a truck and then rear-ended by another vehicle. Had to cut her out. Definite broken wrist. She's having trouble breathing and has been going in and out of consciousness. Said we needed to call a Tara. Police have already called."

Eric's head jerked up and looked at David before looking back at the stretcher being pushed down the hall. "I'll take her. Trauma room two."

Time suddenly transformed to slow-motion as David watched Eric move alongside the gurney with the nurse and EMT. His eyes locked with Eric's as they wheeled her into the room. For the briefest moment, David looked at the woman. Even with the cuts, the blood and the mask, he knew *that* face—the face that had once brought him his only happiness.

Feeling weak, he sat down on the chair near the front desk. He didn't hear the noise, the voices, or the monitors beeping. His world was silent as he tried to comprehend what he'd just witnessed.

He looked toward the trauma room where she was taken. She was the one he had lost, the one who didn't want to be found.

How many times had he re-lived their time together, regretting what had happened and how much pain he had caused everyone—including himself?

Chapter 2

Twenty Years Earlier

Jillian O'Malley sat on Tara Spencer's feet and counted, "Thirty-three, thirty-four, and thirty-five. Come on Tara, fifteen more sit-ups to go."

"I think I'd rather *throw* up on you. You are Satan in disguise. If you let me stop now, I promise never to eat another whole bag of chips at one sitting."

Tara panted while she tried to do another sit-up. "I don't know how you can do a hundred of these. Oh wait, I remember…because you are paid the big bucks to model swimsuits for *The Style*, while I'm the friend sitting on the sideline. By the way, I'm not so sure of the new posters they have hanging in the store at the mall. You don't look natural in that ugly hat." Tara sat up straight.

"Hey, you're the one who wanted to do this. I seem to remember I was the one who wanted to go shopping. Now come on, you have eleven more and you're done. You want to look hot for Keith. Isn't that what you said?"

"You know there are times when I wish they hadn't paired us up as freshman roommates. Why did I have to get you, the model with the perfect figure? I so wish you gained and kept the freshman fifteen instead of passing yours on to me. It's not right that I have the extra pounds for both of us."

Jillian shook her head. "Admit it, I am the only one who can put up with your quirkiness. Plus you've got all the curves and sexiness I'm not allowed to have."

"Yeah, that's me." Tara grinned, pushing her long, naturally white-blonde hair from her face.

Jillian had been nervous four years ago when she started at University of Kentucky. Having taken a year out for modeling, she was a year older than all the other freshman.

On that first day, in walked a bodacious blonde with a big smile and personality to match. On top of it, Tara had a natural sex appeal that attracted men to her like moths to a flame.

After another sit-up, Tara pointed a finger at Jillian. "I just figured it out. Ben broke up with you, didn't he? When people are dumped, they typically drink, eat, sleep, or mope around. Not you. You shop. So spit it out. Tell me what happened."

"You have eight more to go, and then I'll tell."

Tara wiped the sweat off her brow and said, "No, you won't. I know you better. What was it? You wouldn't put out?"

Jillian's shoulders dropped. It was the same reason for all her breakups.

"I'm sorry, Jilly." She continued doing her sit-ups. "Ben was a record so far. Four weeks. Not bad."

"He said I should be flattered to have him as my first," Jillian said when Tara finished her last sit-up.

"Well, isn't he just full of himself?" Tara said between gasps of air. "I think I'm going to have a heart attack right here. Okay, don't take this wrong, but how can someone with smarts and looks like you, be such a klutz when it comes to dating?"

"Maybe I was meant to be single. You know there are more women in this world than men."

"And maybe I'll be abducted by aliens tomorrow. Jeez, Jilly. Can't you come up with anything better than that?"

"Remember, I don't have the sexiness."

Tara crossed her arms over her shapely chest and narrowed her brown eyes. "I swear, how can you be so insecure around men? Gawd, look at you in some of these photo shoots, you have sizzling hot men with you."

"You know most of them are gay, right?"

"Don't care. If I were in your shoes, I'd take my clothes off and ask them to get naked with me."

Jillian was tired of hearing about her appearance. When she looked in the mirror all she saw was the piercing green eyes and sharp nose she got from her Irish father, and the high cheekbones and other facial features of her Native American mother.

It had been "her exotic look" that had captured the attention of the modeling agency head when she and her father had attended the Kentucky Derby back when she was in high school. From then on she modeled, becoming one of the faces for the clothing store *The Style*, as well as appearing in a number of magazines.

Tara attempted another sit-up. "If there was anyone in this world who is meant to be single forever, it's me. I seriously don't think I could be happy with one man, when there are so many out there."

After some silence, she continued. "You're the one destined to meet Mr. All-American, have the perfect family with perfect teeth, white picket fence, and a dog.

I'll be the favorite aunt who comes to do fun things with them, like take them out for junk food and candy."

"Yeah, right," Jillian replied, standing up. "First I have to meet a man and have sex with him."

****

Jillian stood outside on the green and breathed in the crisp November air. There was enough of a breeze to cause the last of the orange and red leaves hanging on the trees to fall. It was not chilly enough to prevent the throngs of students from pouring out of the buildings into the brisk air to soak up the last of the fall sun. Whereas others were sitting on blankets and some playing touch football, Jillian and Tara used this time to exercise—to clear their minds before locking themselves away for the rest of the evening to study.

Plus, she had to continuously exercise to keep her figure lean and toned for the cameras. Tara's sole reason for exercising was to attract the attention of the opposite sex.

Once they were thoroughly warmed up, they silently started their jog. Jillian was lost in her thoughts of never having a steady boyfriend and being a virgin at graduation. Why couldn't she loosen up and be more like Tara, who threw caution to the wind?

Her thoughts were broken into when Tara's elbow hit hers. Jillian looked ahead to see two men running, with headphones perched on their heads. She and Tara liked to guess what music was playing on runners' headsets. Jillian decided the one on the left had to be listening to rock. His head bounced to a distinct beat.

She continued to watch the two men. They were both tall. The lanky one, on the left, bobbed his sandy-haired head and looked ready to trip over his own feet.

The one on the right had darker hair and was more built. Both looked straight ahead, oblivious to her and Tara's fast approach.

Her friend signaled her to pick up the pace to pass the two runners. Jillian chuckled to herself. She knew Tara wanted them to gawk at her backside and hips. Men fell for her curvy figure. Tara! Always the flirt. When Tara was done, one of them would be phoning her.

As they neared, Tara yelled, "Yoo-hoo, passing on the right."

Jillian was near enough that she could hear the music playing over the headphones, so as to know they hadn't heard Tara's sultry words. Jillian started to come up on the right side of the two guys and was shocked to see, out of the corner of her eye, Tara was not following her; she was running right between the two startled men.

The one on the right started to veer to make room, completely unaware Jillian was coming up on that same side. It was inevitable, they were going to smash up. She tried slowing, but it was too late. It was a hard collision. She saw the surprise on his face when he realized he'd run into her. Though he tried to buffer the fall, they went down in a heap in the leaf-littered grass.

She landed on her side with him sprawled on top of her. As quickly as they landed, he immediately sat up, grabbing her hand to help her. Sitting upright, she stared into the most intense blue eyes she'd ever seen. And she had seen plenty, but not like these.

Summoning her courage, without taking her eyes from his, she asked, "Are you okay?"

He stammered, "Y-yeah."

"Good." She felt a smile spread slowly across her face. "You know, there's got to be a less painful way to get my attention than running into me and sitting on my foot." She scrunched her nose, not caring for once if it caused wrinkles. "In case you're wondering. I'm okay, too. But my foot would probably feel better if you weren't sitting on it."

Embarrassed, he immediately stood. Since he was still holding her hand, he pulled her with him. She was nearly his height.

"Uh, sorry, about that. I didn't realize you were next to me. I'm, um, really sorry," he mumbled.

She felt her stomach fluttering. She didn't want him to leave. She was just mobilizing some tenacity. Still grinning, she said, "No harm done. You can always buy me a beer later if you're really sorry."

She glimpsed his companion poke him in the back. Something made her feel flattered that he wouldn't look away from her. While this sometimes happened when guys talked to her, she always had the feeling they really were mentally undressing her. This was different. He was just looking at her face.

"By the way, I'm Jillian. Jillian O'Malley. And if you release my hand, I'll introduce you to my roommate."

She detected a blush before he let go of her hand. He looked uncomfortable.

She gestured toward Tara. "This is Tara Spencer. And you are...?"

His lanky friend immediately extended his hand to Jillian. "Eric Laughlin. And this is David Rainier." He leaned forward and loudly whispered, "You'll have to excuse him, he's a little shy."

David still didn't say anything.

Eric turned to Tara whose arms were folded over her large chest watching everyone with great amusement. Typical.

"He-ey," Tara drawled, trying to be more seductive than usual.

Great, now Tara will turn on the flirt-machine, and they'll both fall for her provocative ways and husky voice.

Jillian turned back to David. *Poor guy*, she thought. She could so easily relate to being at a loss for words. When she looked at his face, she tried to ease the tension by casually shrugging her shoulders.

She rested her hand on his arm and said, "Listen, we've gotta go. Nice meeting you, David Rainer. I meant what I said earlier. Meet me at Gilly's tonight for that beer." With that, she gave the signal to Tara, and they took off, waving a goodbye over their shoulders.

Chapter 3

Eric and David watched the girls run. Both had a fluid stride; both ponytails swung in unison. At the end of the green, they veered off to the dorms.

Eric looked over at him. "You know the blonde was the one who was dressed up as Madonna at that Halloween party."

"Uh-huh," David responded, not being able to get the image of Jillian's smile from his mind.

"Wasn't the dark-haired one the girl that Dan was googly-eyed over?"

"Yep."

Eric continued with amusement in his voice, "I think that went pretty well, don't you?"

David shot him the look. "Going real well until you opened your big mouth to say I was shy. Talk about humiliation!"

"Well, someone had to say something, and I didn't hear any words coming from your mouth. You just stood there not letting go of her hand. Are we going to Gilly's tonight?"

"Nope, after classes tomorrow, I have to work at the hospital until two in the morning."

"What? Are you crazy? Are you really going to turn down an invitation from one of the hottest girls on campus? Wait until I tell Dan. He'll run over there now, wait for her to arrive, and then follow her around like a love-sick puppy."

"I'm not going. And you're not telling Dan."

"What's so wrong with going out and having fun once in awhile? It's not going to kill you. I'll make you a deal. We'll walk over, have a beer with them, and then leave. 'Cause, I wanna get to know Tara. Did you see the hooters on her?"

He may as well agree because his roommate wasn't about to give up. "Fine, one hour, and no one tells Dan, or Cathy, about this. I don't need to hear it from either of them."

****

Gilly's wasn't very crowded. The usual patrons sat at their tables. As time passed, more students from the campus made their way into the bar. Every time the door opened, Jillian glanced over to scope out the new arrivals.

Josh came to sit in the chair recently vacated by Tara, who was on the dance floor. He moved the chair close to hers, signaling he had something to tell her and didn't want other ears to hear. She pushed her long, black hair behind her ears and bent close to him to listen. Once he began his tale, she ignored the doorway and all who entered.

Typical of a Josh story, mostly because he kept repeating himself, the woes over his latest lover began to drag.

Jillian glanced up, and her heart stopped. *He* was here! He was sitting at the bar, talking with the guy he had been running with earlier. She no longer heard anything Josh said.

She felt as if she was in a surreal dream where everything around her was silent. She studied his "too-defined" face, as Tara had called it when they got back to the dorm. She found those features masculine and attractive. His piercing eyes were deep-set and serious. She watched as he looked intently into his listener's face. His mouth was hard, and the muscles appeared tense. His dark brown hair had a slight wave. She had an urge to run her fingers through it.

He stopped talking and looked her way. He had caught her staring at him. She felt her pulse quicken. In the middle of Josh's sentence, she picked up her bag and excused herself from the table to thread her way to the bar. She was on a mission, and no one was going to stop her. She was drawn to this guy like a magnet.

She stood next to David and said, "I was about ready to give up on you. I was giving it to the end of Josh's story before I made my exit." Biting her lip, she looked over her shoulder at Josh. "Come to think of it, I never heard the end of his story."

Jillian couldn't pull her eyes away from David's deep blue ones. He was freshly shaved, and the scent of his aftershave invigorated her senses. She felt herself leaning forward to smell him. He wore a pair of old jeans and a white cotton button-down shirt. He looked like the classic college student.

It was subtle, but she noticed the nod David gave to his friend to leave. Eric slid off the bar stool and headed toward Tara on the dance floor. *Poor guy. Smitten with a flirt like Tara.* Setting her empty glass on the sticky counter, Jillian jumped onto the empty stool before anyone could snag it.

"Do you want another one?" he asked her.

His voice was rich and deep. All she could think of was velvety chocolate.

"Are you saying you're sorry for running me over?" she asked quietly. She could feel the corners of her lips curl into a smile—the one she gave the cameras.

He put his finger up. "Now, wait a minute. I didn't run over you. I think we can say your friend *made* me bump into you, which made you fall. So, what are you drinking?"

She was going to have fun with this. "First, are you sorry?"

His eyes bored deeper into hers. She saw the mischief in them as he answered. "Nope."

"Well then, you can't buy me a drink until you are." By now, the bartender had come over and stood in front of them. She looked at him and said politely, "I will have sparkling water, please." She looked at David's near-empty bottle. "He'll have another."

The bartender filled a glass with sparking water and handed it to her. "On the house." He opened up another beer bottle and set it on the counter.

"Thanks, Larry."

Jillian looked at David and held her glass in the air to him. "Well, you got off the hook tonight. When you decide you're sorry, I'll let you buy me that beer." She could feel her closed mouth grinning from ear to ear.

"I think it may be awhile."

"Stubborn, aren't you?" She flipped her hair over her shoulders.

"Maybe. So, what are you studying?"

You, she wanted to say, but knew that sounded too flirtatious. It hit her! That was something Tara would say. Maybe after all these years she was finally learning.

He was waiting for her answer. It wasn't a hard question, yet her mouth wouldn't cooperate. Finally, she found the words she needed and told him about her major, and her classes.

Something in her brain snapped and, guiltily, she asked about him. She could listen to his deep voice all night. Between that and his eyes, she felt like she was being hypnotized. Her trance was broken when he stopped talking and looked over at Tara and Eric standing next to them.

In her sultry voice, Tara asked, "Are you ready to go? I need to get back and get some sleep."

Jillian watched Tara eye-bat a few times and then feign a yawn. Always the drama queen.

She looked back at David, who was watching Tara. Men were always captivated by her. He turned back to Jillian. "Do you have to go, too?" he asked.

"I need to," she answered. She would rather stay here with him but dared not say so.

Eric jumped in. "We'll walk you home." He motioned his thumb toward David. "Plus, this one can get cranky if he stays out too late."

Jillian watched David wince at his friend's teasing words. She rested her hand on top of his. Looking into his eyes, she quietly said, "I'd like that."

Eric and Tara walked ahead. Tara's arm looped in Eric's, as if they were already a couple. They chattered as they walked.

She glanced over at David who was walking a safe distance from her. He remained silent. She figured he didn't want to provide his friend with more ribbing ammo and felt sorry for him.

As they neared the dorms, Eric and Tara stopped to

wait for them. Jillian sighed as Eric dramatically kissed Tara's hand good night. Wishing her a good night, David shook hers.

It was a start. Or so she hoped.

Chapter 4

Jillian was beyond angry as she left Dr. Neilson's office—so mad that she wanted to scream and kick something.

Dr. Neilson, her professor of Adolescent Psychology, always made her nervous. She had met with him to review the draft of her final paper. He had flipped through her notes and outline, making snorting sounds, like a pig rooting through food. It seemed an appropriate analogy since his office had the musty smell of old garbage.

With a seemingly disgusted look, he tossed the papers back to Jillian, glaring at her with his beady black eyes. His voice was condescending as he spoke. "Ms. O'Malley, I don't know why you're wasting my time with this. What you have here is weak and unorganized. Did you put this together five minutes ago? That's what it looks like to me."

Jillian thought her head was going to explode off her shoulders. She wanted to pick up her bag and hit him. Instead, with forced politeness, she said, "I put *a lot* of time into this."

This paper was half of her semester grade, and she needed this class to graduate in the spring.

"Well, I suggest you put in more. Perhaps you could focus less on which magazine your face will appear in next. Goodbye."

Jillian couldn't move. All she could do was stare at this insulting man. Maybe she didn't hear the words correctly. This was discrimination. She wished she could be like Tara, who'd flip him the finger, tell him where to go, and what he could do while he was there.

"Did you not understand me, Ms. O'Malley? I've things to do, so kindly close the door on your way out."

She gathered her papers from his cluttered desk, stuffed them into her bag, and left his office.

As it was chilly, she pulled her cream-colored hat further down as she headed to the library. She didn't look at the students walking to and from the buildings for their late-afternoon classes. All she could see was Dr. Nielson's sneer. How she wanted to flush him down a toilet!

Jillian took the stairs to the fifth floor of the library where the books she needed were kept. She'd stay there all night, if necessary. Tomorrow she would go to her counselor, Dr. Allen, and lay out everything before him. He would listen and offer guidance.

She went to an isolated table in the corner nearest the window and threw her coat in the chair next to her. She left her hat on, hoping no one would recognize her. From the shelves she pulled all the books needed to finish her paper. She sat facing the window with her back to the rest of library.

For the next several hours, she continued working. She didn't dare look at her watch. Right now time was her enemy. As the minutes ticked by, there was less movement of books, papers, and students. Jillian read what she had put together. It did sound better than her earlier presentation. Maybe that was it. Maybe Dr. Neilson knew she had potential, and that was his way of pushing her. Then she remembered his exact words and was angry all over again.

Standing up, she slammed the books shut and piled them on top of each other. Cursing her professor under her breath, she lifted the seven books to put them on the return cart. Misjudging where the corner of the table was, she dropped them all.

"Dammit, shit, shit, dammit," she shouted. "I hate this, and all men!"

Bending down to pick up the scattered books, she froze. David, of all people, was sitting at the next table with a look of disbelief. Even in an old blue UK sweatshirt, she found him appealing.

For the last week-and-a-half, she had tried, in vain, to get his attention when she saw him. He was always too preoccupied to pay any attention to her. Now, after witnessing her tantrum, she was sure he'd purposely avoid her at all costs.

She picked up the books, glad that her long hair shielded her hot, embarrassed face. *Why does he have to be here?* She was mortified and wondered if there was a way to slither out of the library unnoticed. Barring that, perhaps an earthquake could come and only she would fall into its chasm.

Holding all the books, she dared to look over at him. He was still sitting there watching her. He probably thought she was a nutcase.

Facing him square on, she asked, "You didn't see any of that, did you?"

"Nope."

"Good." She walked past him with her stack of books.

He was wearing the same aftershave as the night at

the bar.

She had to get out of there. Glancing at her watch, she decided that if she slowly returned the books to their shelves, instead of the cart, maybe he'd be gone when she returned. It was a plan.

With the pile of books in her arms, she glanced in his direction. He was bent over his own set of books.

She dawdled, walking up and down the aisles, replacing the borrowed books to their rightful places. She stopped at the end of the aisle to peer around the corner. He was still sitting at the table studying. She focused on *willing* him to leave.

"I know you're there," he said in a deep whispered voice. "The library's open for another half hour, and I'm not ready to go."

How humiliating! She could feel the heat return to her face.

She came out of the aisle with her head held high and sat down in the chair next to him. Not looking into his face, she twirled the ends of her hair in her fingers. "So, how clumsy did I look?"

"Very. But it was entertaining." He stopped, trying to suppress a smile.

She evil-eyed him and groaned. This could not get any worse.

"You know, if you're going to become a teacher, you may want to come up with a more acceptable string of curse words." With that, he began to laugh.

She looked up at him and realized he wasn't going to stop. The few times she had seen him he had been so serious. Now, he was actually trying to be funny, and at her expense.

She said, "Well, aren't you a regular comedian?

Are you taking this show on the road?"

"Well, I'd need you to open with that little act of yours."

At that comment, she punched his upper arm.

Becoming thoughtful, he asked, "You want to tell me what happened to put you in such a mood?"

Reluctantly, she told him what had transpired earlier that afternoon. She confided that sometimes she hated that people couldn't see past her exterior to what was on the inside. She hated how people thought she didn't have a brain. "I'm going to surprise all of them. Not only will I be a great teacher, but I'm going to be a principal."

She stopped suddenly, noticing David hadn't uttered a single word. Still twirling her hair, she bit her bottom lip before popping the question, "Are you ever going to ask me out on a date?"

The look on his face told her he was as shocked by her query as she was for asking it. He remained silent, his eyes searching hers for answers she didn't have.

She continued, "Ever since we met, I've tried to flirt with you. But you seem to avoid me like the plague. I've come up with several possible reasons for this." Jillian lifted her fingers to count. "Number one, you're already seeing someone—probably that really beautiful girl with the hideous glasses who is always at your side. Number two, you're gay. Or three, you're not interested because I'm not your type."

She stopped and looked at her fingers and then back at him. "Wait, there is a fourth. You're also training to be a priest and have taken an oath of celibacy. That's it, isn't it?"

Leaning close to her, he whispered, "Nope."

She matched his gesture and moving toward him so their noses were almost touching, whispered back, "What is it, then?"

She stared at his slightly-parted lips. Her breathing became shallow and uneven. Before she knew it, he put his hands on the sides of her face and pressed his warm lips, ever so gently, to hers. Every hair on her body tingled, and goose bumps ran down her back.

He pulled away slightly from her, their noses still touching.

Looking into his intense blue eyes, she felt herself being drawn into their pools.

He wrapped his hand behind her neck and pulled her back to him. Now, he kissed her hard until she opened her mouth. When their tongues touched, there was an explosion inside her. She could feel the blood rushing through and pounding in her ears. Their tongues moved together. She put her hands to his face and ran them through his thick hair.

She loved the taste of him and couldn't let go. Her body was responding to him. Her heart was beating loud, and she was sure everyone in the library could hear it.

The moment was broken when they heard the sound of someone clearing their throat. They pulled apart. The assistant librarian stood behind them, tapping his foot on the floor. "This is not the appropriate place for that," he said in a high-pitched clip. "May I remind you the library is about to close, and you both need to leave?"

They looked at each other, smiling at being caught.

Jillian stood up, brushed her fingers to her lips, and stared at David. Her mind was in knots. She walked slowly to her table to retrieve her bag. She was quiet and couldn't think. Something unexplainable had happened to her. Her body was warm all over. She was aching for him to kiss her again. She looked over her shoulder to see him pulling on his jacket. He loaded his backpack before hoisting it onto his shoulder.

He helped her with her coat and took her hand while they silently walked out of the library into the cold night air. His hand was strong, engulfing hers. The campus was quiet, but for a few students walking on the green.

Once outside, Jillian said to him, "You didn't answer me in there."

David grinned back at her, "I think I did."

She knitted her eyebrows together and thought awhile. "No. No, I don't think you did."

"I suppose you're right. I have a rule that I won't allow myself to get involved with someone until I'm done with medical school."

"Why is that?" she asked.

"Because, between working and studying, I don't have a lot of free time." He stopped walking and pointed back to the library they had just exited. "I'm worried if I spend a lot of time with you, I won't be able to focus on my studies."

She felt as if the air had been knocked out of her. What had happened to her with that kiss had never happened before. *Ever.* She wanted more. She wanted to feel the warm rush through her, the hair on the top of her head tingling and standing up. She wanted to feel the smoothness of his skin beneath her fingertips. Did he not realize that?

Well, she was not going to let him push her away.

She needed to talk with Tara. She'd know what to do.

They resumed their walking.

Jillian was looking straight ahead into the night and said, "You know, you lied back there. You must have *some* free time." At his raised eyebrow, she continued. "I know for a fact, you run."

"That's to get the oxygen to my head to—"

She stopped and turned to face him, never letting go of his hand. David's cheeks were red from the cold air. "Yeah, yeah, yeah. Will you please let me finish?"

"Sorry."

"Since you're human, you must find time to eat, sleep, and shower. Right?"

"Are you asking to join me?" His grin was devilish.

"Yes. No!" She stammered and started to bite her lip. "Don't confuse the issue here. Let me put it this way. No one can kiss like that without having had some practice. So you obviously have dated, right?"

She waited. "Are you going to answer me?"

"I thought I was letting you finish."

With her hand still in his, she turned and started to walk. "You know what I mean. Don't try to avoid the question. Just answer it. I don't think it's that hard."

"I don't know what to say. I've dated here and there. Are you happy now?"

She shook her head and didn't respond.

In front of her dormitory, she stopped and looked up at him. "If you aren't interested, all you have to do is say so. Don't try to soften it by saying you are too busy. Just be honest and say it."

She returned his stare with an angry glare.

He adjusted the knap sack on his shoulder.

Cupping her face in both of his hands, he kissed her.

It was a hard kiss that she felt wanted and demanded more. She sucked in her breath and pushed her body into his, giving into the heat of passion.

He pressed her against him as his mouth explored hers. Suddenly, and without warning, he ended it, leaving her wanting more. "Goodnight, Jillian."

"Ugh! You drive me crazy. You know that? Absolutely crazy. I'm not even going to tell you goodnight because you don't deserve it."

She walked to the entrance of the dorm and punched in the code to open the door. Before slamming the door behind her, she turned toward him. "You *still* owe me that beer."

He nodded and waved before starting his walk across the green to graduate housing.

She thought he looked lonely walking in the dark night.

In her dorm room, Jillian undressed quietly, without lights, so as not to wake Tara. Listening to Tara's breathing, she knew she was asleep and not pretending. Crawling into bed, she felt a crinkle on her pillow. She didn't have to read it to know it was a note from Tara asking where she had been. She lay there staring at the ceiling. Wild, outgoing Tara was always worried about her.

Her thoughts drifted to David. Just remembering his kisses made her feel warm all over. His words, however, confused her. *Why was he scared?* She'd ask her roommate, who was dating his roommate. Her last thoughts before falling asleep were that she and Tara's next mission would be to score a date with David.

Chapter 5

The next day at lunch in the cafeteria, Jillian observed several medical students walking past. Tara immediately waved to Eric and gave him a seductive wink. Jillian knew they would be hooking up this weekend, with her gone at a modeling shoot.

David walked by, without acknowledging or even looking in her direction. *Jerk*! Immediately, she focused on her salad, spearing the spinach leaves with her fork.

Without attracting the attention of anyone at the table, especially Tara, she glanced his way from the corner of her eye. He was facing her, as he often did, but appeared to be engrossed in conversation with the guy sitting across from him.

She quickly looked away and turned toward Josh and Julia's debate of school politics. Listening to their banter would, surely, take her mind away from her inner turmoil.

Josh and Julia departed, still arguing over whether the appointment of the new Dean of Students was a good thing. Tara grabbed the salad plate away from her. "You goin' to tell me what's goin' on? Or do we have to play twenty questions?"

"Nothin'. Zip."

"And I'm the Queen of England. Why are you not bowing before me?" Tara shook her long, blonde hair. "You're such a liar. First, you get all sullen. And then you attack your salad as if it's going to mysteriously come alive and attempt to crawl off the plate."

Folding her arms, Tara sat back in her chair, waiting impatiently for an answer. "Come on, spit it out. And I don't mean the carrot that you're taking your sweet time chewing. It should be liquefied by now."

After finally swallowing her food, Jillian propped her elbows on the table to rest her forehead in both her hands. "It's useless. Finally, I meet someone I'm attracted to. I try to flirt with him, and I get no reaction whatsoever."

"So, move on. There are bigger fish in the sea."

"But I'm not interested in bigger fish. I found a good-sized one but can't seem to catch it."

"Does he want to be caught?"

"I don't know."

Her elbows still on the table, Jillian confided to her best friend, "Last night when David walked me back from the library, he kissed me like I've never been kissed before. It was absolutely wonderful. I heard angels sing. And then, just as suddenly as they appeared, the heavenly choir was gone…and he was wishing me a good night."

Tara dramatically put her arms up in the air and leaned forward. "Whoa, whoa, whoa! Wait a minute. You never told me this, Jillian Margaret O'Malley. You only said you saw him at the library and made a complete ass out of yourself when you hit the corner of the table. There was never any mention of a goodnight kiss."

"I haven't had the chance to tell you." She leaned forward and motioned for Tara to do the same. "First we got caught kissing in the library. He was the one who initiated it. It was wonderful. So much better than Ben."

"Really? I thought you said Ben's Val Kilmer lips were amazing."

"David was better. Much better. Not to mention that Ben had this creepy thing about kissing in front of mirrors so he could watch himself."

"Are you serious?" Tara asked incredulously.

"Yep." Jillian pulled her plate of salad back in front of her. She put the last of the spinach in her mouth, before continuing. "Also, in Child Psy class this morning, Ben told me that he knew I was a virgin. He wants to be my first so I will always have something to compare others to."

"What!" Tara's mouth hung open. "So what did you tell him?"

"I told him if I slept with him, then I'd be starting on the bottom and working my way up." Jillian whined, "Do you know I probably will be the only female in the history of this school to walk across the graduation stage a virgin. How depressing is that?"

"You know you can pay someone, to avoid that embarrassment." Tara began her loud, throaty laugh. Students at nearby tables glanced at them.

Jillian's eyes darted to David. He was looking in their direction. Now, she couldn't tell if he was looking at her or at the person sitting across from him. She felt her heart begin to beat faster. She rested her elbow on the table, set her chin in her palm, and once again, glanced in David's direction. "Admit it. Don't you think he has a certain magnetism?"

Tara glanced over at him as she popped a potato chip into her mouth, "Nope."

"You know what I'd do if he ever did ask me on a date? I'd do a cartwheel to celebrate."

Tara's face was blank. "A cartwheel? You are sometimes *not right*."

"Look who's calling the kettle black," Jillian countered.

"I'd only do a cartwheel if you slept with someone. However, if you want my opinion, I think the girl sitting next to him is his bedmate. Look at the way she looks at him and how close to him she sits. There's obviously some familiarity between those two. She could be real pretty if she didn't wear those ugly glasses. It's as if she wants to look like a Plain Jane, when it's obvious she not. So, back to my point. We need to find some other poor soul—"

"Poor soul?"

"Yes, someone who will fall head over heels for the lovely Jillian *and* be willing to get his heart broken."

Tara was probably right. The girl sat next to David whenever he was in the cafeteria. She was probably the reason Jillian couldn't attract his attention. There was a definite beauty hidden behind those ghastly glasses. Plus, she and David probably had some medical school classmate connection she could not compete with.

The few times Jillian had dated, she'd been bored. Usually she was not invited on a second one once she made it clear she wasn't interested in immediate sex. David intrigued her. The two times she had been with him, he didn't seem sophomorically eager to get her into bed.

After a period of silence, Tara said, "You know, dating isn't supposed to be hard or require this much work. I think—"

"You're right. I shouldn't waste my time or energy. However, I have to say, that kiss…" She sighed. "Aah!…it was something else—a kiss that made me think of getting naked with him."

Tara was silent for a few seconds before looking at Jillian with a Cheshire Cat grin. In a very low, barely audible, voice she said, "Will you let me finish? I think we need to launch *Operation: Virgin Extinction*."

****

On Friday afternoon, there seemed to be more people than usual in the cafeteria. The noise level was high. Tara and Jillian sat at their usual table waiting for Josh and Julia to arrive. David and Eric stood in the sandwich line laughing about something. "Glasses," as Jillian and Tara were now calling her, with her brown hair pulled back severely from her face was standing next to them. She appeared annoyed by the subject of the men's laughter.

David and Glasses made their way to the far corner table and sat with the other medical students. Eric approached Jillian and Tara's table, leaned down, and whispered something into Tara's ear. She giggled and shook her head at whatever had been said for her ears only. He stood up and carried his tray to join David.

Jillian asked, "What was that all about?"

With a wicked smile, Tara replied, "He wanted to make sure we were still on for tonight and tomorrow since you're not going to be around."

Jillian's shoulders sagged knowing her roommate was going to spend most of the day in bed while she had to work. She could only shake her head.

"Don't you ever get bored, having sex all the

time?"

"No. Once you experience it, and you will, if everything goes right, you'll want it all the time." She stopped to sip on her Diet Coke. "Just want to let you know that Glasses is sitting next to The Target, eating his french fries. Uh-oh, he must have said something, because she is pouting. Now she's put her arm around his shoulders."

Hearing that, there was no way Jillian could pull this off. She'd make an utter fool of herself.

"Stop biting your lip, will you? They're not going to like it tomorrow if you show up with a fat lip. They'll send you home, and my fun will be ruined." Tara leaned forward to whisper. "Now, all you have to do is get between Glasses and The Target and do your thing. I'll stay here and monitor the situation, then meet up with you outside to let you know what happens. Now go, before Glasses eats all of his food and ends up sitting in his lap."

After swinging her book bag over her shoulder, Jillian stood and threaded her way to David's table. She pretended she was at work and held her head high. She wore the smile she had perfected for the cameras. She conjured a photographer saying, "Come on, Jillian. Give us that smile. You know the one...ah...perfect." Inside, however, she was trembling.

Halfway there, David took note of her and stopped eating. She never took her eyes from him. His head turned as she came up behind him. She quickly shot Eric a glance, certain he knew what she was about to do.

Jillian came to a stop next to David. She leaned down, so her head was between him and Glasses. She flipped her long, black hair over her shoulder, hoping some of the strands would hit the competition. She put her mouth close enough to his ear that he would feel her lips moving.

In a loud whisper so everyone could hear she said, "I'm heading out because I've gotta work all day tomorrow. I wanted to make sure we're still on for Sunday night. Six-thirty in front of the student union, right?"

His puzzled face turned to stare into her eyes. Tara's plan seemed to be working.

Before he could say anything, she gently placed her hand on the side of his face and passionately kissed him. The silence at every table in the vicinity was overwhelming.

Jillian straightened up, and just as she'd practiced with Tara, she said seductively, "See you then."

Once again, she held her head high and walked across the room making sure to sway her hips. She really wanted to skip with glee out of the room, but that would've been too obvious. She needed to appear poised and confident. As she opened the door, she glanced back at David. All who'd witnessed this event were stunned. Her gaze swept across the room to Tara and Josh. They gave her a thumbs-up. She had won round one. She saw it in their faces.

Chapter 6

The taste of snow was in the air on Sunday evening. A sense of excitement was shared among the few students milling about in front of the student union. They were hoping for a snowstorm to cancel classes tomorrow.

After walking over with Jillian, Tara and Eric went inside to get hot chocolate. She remained outside waiting for David, constantly checking her watch. It was almost six-thirty, and she was getting nervous, though Eric told her there was no reason to be. She sincerely hoped he would show up, knowing she was there. But would he? Surely, he'd come, or she would be a laughing-stock tomorrow.

A group of students walked by and greeted her. She responded to their hellos but immediately returned her gaze toward graduate housing. A lone figure sat on a bench across the street. She strained her eyes but couldn't quite make out whom the person was. Was he watching her?

She peeked at her watch again. On the verge of panic, she bit her cold lips and pulled her red wool coat closer around her. She turned to face the student union to kick a pretend rock. She sensed him behind her before she heard him.

There was amusement in his deep, baritone voice. "How many times were you going to check your watch? Walking across the green, I counted three times."

The weight on Jillian's shoulders slipped away. She took a step toward him to wrap her arms behind his neck. She tasted his cold lips and minty breath. His arms went around her waist and pulled their bodies close. She didn't want to let him go, even when she heard Tara clearing her throat. She kept her mouth against his.

"Will you two get a room already?" asked Tara. "Come on, let's get going or we'll be late."

Once their bodies separated, Tara handed each of them a large cup filled with hot chocolate. "This was to keep you warm, but after what I just saw, I doubt you need it."

Not taking his eyes from Jillian, David asked, "Where are we going on this mystery date?"

Taking his hand in hers, Jillian answered, "To watch *It's a Wonderful Life*. Don't you know, every Sunday in December a holiday movie is shown in the auditorium? We need to get going so we get a good seat."

As they walked together, Tara turned and commented. "You need to clear your calendar for next Sunday. They're showing her other favorite, *A Christmas Carol*. You'll want to get there early as she likes to be first in line so she doesn't miss a minute of the movie, though it always ends the same way."

Still holding hands and clutching their cups in the other, they walked the rest of the way in silence. Jillian had an odd feeling someone was watching them. At one point, she stopped to look behind her, but there was no one.

Waiting in line, David told them about working in the Emergency Room that weekend. He had them laughing when he shared the story about putting stitches in an elderly woman who was insistent that he was her husband.

"Do you want to be an ER doctor, then?" Jillian asked.

"Not at all. I want to specialize in Cardiology."

When the line started to move into the auditorium, he and Eric continued to share hospital stories. Once inside, Jillian and Tara took the cups of hot chocolate and went to secure seats while Eric and David got popcorn.

Jillian glanced at Tara, "I had the weirdest feeling that someone was following us when we walked over here."

Tara nodded and before sipping her hot chocolate said, "It was Glasses."

"Oh." Jillian nodded, not feeling good about this.

When the movie ended, Tara and Eric said their goodbyes and started walking back to the dorms. Over her shoulder, Tara mouthed the words, "take your time" to Jillian.

She wanted to laugh. Even though the two had all weekend alone together, they still needed more? Jillian winked at them.

"What was that all about?" David asked, looking at her.

"Nothing." She turned back to David with a knowing smile. "Do you want to grab something to eat? I'm a little hungry. There was hardly any popcorn in the bag you got."

He shook his head at her. "That's because someone

tossed more than they ate. I'm sure the janitors are going to love cleaning up after you."

She caught hold of his hand. "Come on, let's go to Max's and grab a sandwich. I'm hungry, and I can't go back to my room right away. The lovebirds need more alone time, if you know what I mean."

Softly, he said, "If you want, we can always go back to my room."

Stunned, she didn't know what to say. Was he wanting to sleep with her, or were his intentions more innocent? She bit her lip thinking on how to respond.

As if reading her mind, he said, "It's not want you think, Jillian. I thought we could just sit and talk."

Realizing she had been holding her breath, she sighed and said, "Do you mind if we grab a sandwich instead?"

In the silence of the cold night, they walked the several streets to Max's. Jillian felt the warm air hit her cold face as they entered. David's cheeks and nose were red from the cold air.

She suggested, "How about we split a ham and cheese sandwich? I don't think I can eat a whole one."

When he nodded, she gave the order to the bored student behind the counter. She immediately reached into her pocket to pull out money. Seeing the look on his face, she said, "My treat. I'm the one who asked you out on this date. Plus, I'm still waiting on that beer you owe me, so save your money for that."

The guy took the money from Jillian. She followed David to a table in the back to wait for their hot sandwich.

"Thanks for being a good sport about tonight. I wasn't sure you were going to come," she admitted while he helped her out of her wool coat.

"Why not?" He took off his seen-one-too-many-winter-seasons jacket.

"Ever since that night at the library, you've gone to great lengths to avoid me. Tara said if you weren't going to ask me out, I'd have to make the first move. We worked out that scenario to make you feel almost obligated to come."

Sitting forward in the seat and resting both hands on the table, he responded, "It seems to have worked. How could I say no?"

"I can't believe I actually went through with it. I was sure that you'd not show. Do you regret coming?

"Nope," he answered. "I must say it was a clever plan. However, my buddy, Dan, is a bit deflated. All semester he's been summoning up the courage to ask you out."

"Really! Which one is he?"

The skinny student working the register brought their drinks and sandwich to the table.

"He has the blond curly hair."

"Oh," she said. "I met him during the summer semester. He joined me a few times for lunch. He can talk non-stop. More than Tara." Jillian covered her mouth in embarrassment. "Oops, I'm sorry. I shouldn't have said that. I mean, he's your friend."

"Don't worry about it. You speak the truth."

After taking a huge bite from his sandwich, he asked, "You mentioned you had work. Where's that?"

"Here and there." She nibbled on the corner of the hot ham. Suddenly, she was no longer hungry.

She hated talking about the job that helped her pay for school. People treated her differently once they found out what she did. "Most times, I'm in a studio," she finally said.

"Studio?" He sounded puzzled by her answer.

"I do some modeling." She was a bit anxious waiting for his reaction. Hopefully, he'd be unimpressed.

He snapped his fingers to point at her. "Wait! I heard about you. You're the model for that store at the mall. What's it called?"

"In Style." She watched him.

"Yes. So was it for them that you worked this weekend?"

"No. This weekend it was for Hannaford Jewelers." She held her wrists up to him. "I mean, have you ever seen more perfect wrists on which to perch a diamond bracelet?" she asked sarcastically.

He reached over and gently took one in his hand and said, "Never." He lifted her wrist to his lips and kissed it.

She found that gesture to be both romantic and seductive at the same time. Her whole body went still, as her girl parts woke up.

He continued holding onto her. "I hope you don't mind me saying, but you do have an exotic look. I think it's your eyes and smile together."

"Thank you." She could feel herself blushing. She found statements like this annoying when she worked, but the way he said it was different. "That's what you get when you mix a little Irish blood with Native American."

"You're an Indian?"

"Yep. My real mother was from the Sioux tribe in South Dakota, and for the most part, I favor her coloring and features."

"Real mother? What happened?" he asked.

She appreciated the concern in his voice, but she was uncertain how much to share. "Long story. Maybe, I'll tell you some other time." She pushed her plate in front of him.

"I have time," he said, picking up her sandwich.

"My mother died of breast cancer when I was six. I was too young to understand what was happening. On the day she died, my nana came into my classroom and took me home. A few days later, she packed up my things, and I went to live with her and Grandpa for a year or so."

"Wow. A year?" he asked, picking up his drink.

"My nana told me that my mom and dad were so much in love that her death almost broke him. As Nana tells it, she went over there one day and about kicked him in the 'arse' as she likes to say. Reminded him that he had a daughter that needed him. He was at a loss on what to do, but Nana was there to help him."

"Did he ever remarry?"

"Yeah. Barb. She's the photographer who got me into modeling."

"Really?" he asked incredulously.

"When I was fourteen I was with my dad at the Kentucky Derby. He was the vet-on-call for Bloomfield Stables. They had a horse running that year. I was standing at the stall gate when Barb snapped my picture several times without me knowing. She came over to introduce herself, and I chatted a little bit with her. A few days later, we were called by the modeling agency that she worked for. She and my dad hit it off. She left New York City to marry my dad and become my manager"

"So, is she the evil stepmother?"

"Not really. My dad needed someone. And I needed to make money to help pay for school. My dad had a lot of bills from when my mom died. Heck, there are worse things to do."

Jillian stopped to take a sip of her drink. "So enough about me, what about your family?

"I'm from a little town in eastern Kentucky."

"Oh." Sensing a reluctance to discuss his family, she asked about final exams which were only two weeks away.

Jillian had no idea how long they'd been talking, but too soon the skinny cashier came over to tell them it was closing time. They looked around to see they were the only ones left in the deli. She looked at David and laughed. "I guess we have a way of staying until closing time."

Laughing, he helped her with her coat. Was it her imagination that his hands lingered on her shoulders? She tossed her hair and turned to thank him. Only then did he drop his hands and put them in his pockets.

In the cold, silent outdoors she looped her arm through his for warmth, but more to be close to him. She breathed in the air. "I think it's going to snow. Can't you feel it?"

David looked at her but didn't reply.

"Whatcha doing for holiday break?" she asked.

When he remained silent, she wondered what it was she'd said. "Tara and I'll be at my parents' in Vickery, two towns away, where she'll be working at her co-op job. In January, we're heading out to Utah for skiing. So, what about you?"

"I'll be staying here to work at the hospital," he said quietly

She smiled, glad he wasn't going home.

When they arrived at her building, he pulled her close to kiss her good night.

Goose bumps ran up her spine to the base of her neck. She didn't want it to stop or to let him go. Every time he touched her with his lips and tongue, she could feel a surge of heat racing through her. Jillian was sure, when he touched her, there was enough electricity going through her body that she could light up the entire campus.

Her heart was beating fast, and once he let go of her mouth, she was gasping for air. She looked at him, wanting more. She reached up and ran her gloved fingers over his face.

David grabbed her hand to stop its progress and lowered his mouth back over hers. His mouth and tongue ravished hers. She could feel his demands. She felt his body responding when she leaned into him.

Suddenly, he pulled away. "Goodnight," he said abruptly and turned to walk away.

Confused by his sudden departure, Jillian yelled, "By the way, are you going to go with me next week to see *Christmas Carol*?"

"Wouldn't miss it," David answered, keeping his back to her.

Good, she thought. Smiling inside and out, she walked into the building. She couldn't wait to tell Tara.

Chapter 7

That night snow blanketed the city and campus several inches deep. All morning classes were cancelled. The atmosphere on campus was energized.

When their afternoon classes ended, David suggested to Eric they make a detour by Tara and Jillian's dorm. No sooner were the words out of his mouth than he heard Tara yelling at the top of her lungs from atop a nearby hill. "Eric. Come join us."

She was sitting on a cafeteria tray, sledding down the hill toward them. Whisking past, she fell backward, laughing like a five-year-old. Not far behind her came another sledder shouting, "Move out of the way!"

They jumped back just in time. Cathy and Dan, who had been walking with David and Eric, were sprayed with snow when Jillian skidded to a stop.

She looked up, her cheeks glowing from the cold and the fun. Her eyes were bright and alive. She was laughing and had trouble speaking, "You've...got to...try this. It's too much fun."

Shaking the snow from her glasses and coat, Cathy rolled her eyes and mumbled just loud enough for everyone to hear, "How childish."

Cathy's comment annoyed him, yet David saw that he was the only one who had paid it any attention. The others threw their knapsacks on the nearest clean bench and raced up the hill after Jillian, Tara, and some other students.

At the top of the hill, Jillian handed the tray to David motioning for him to sit on it. He sailed down the hill and came to a stop not far from Cathy. She fixed him with a frosty stare. Wordlessly, he picked up the tray and scurried back to the top of the hill as Eric and Tara, seated together, whisked by him.

He sat on the tray again, calling for Jillian to get on his lap. The closeness of her body to his, when she sat, momentarily unnerved him. He sensed a matching nervousness when her body went strangely still. What was it about her that made him feel this way, made him forget about everything around him?

"Are you ready?" he whispered in her ear. When she nodded, he pushed off and they flew down the hill. He wrapped his arms around her, and she leaned back into him.

After making it to the bottom, neither made any movement to get off the small tray. David couldn't. Something was happening inside him. Though he had known her only a short time, something about her made him feel carefree. He didn't want to let go of that.

The moment's mood came to a sudden end when Eric crashed into them.

David pushed Jillian off his lap and into the snow. He picked up the tray and started running up the hill again. Jillian chased after him, stopping every so often to make another snowball to throw it at him. Soon, a massive snowball fight ensued.

At one point, Jillian came running out of nowhere and tackled him, knocking him to the ground. She sat on his stomach and held her hands over her head in victory, singing, "*We are the Champions. We are the*

Champ—"

"Jillian!" he cried. He had seen the snowball seconds before it hit her full force in the face, knocking her off him.

He reached for her and leveled a gaze at the assailant—Cathy. The look of hatred on her face sent a shudder through him. She pushed her glasses to the bridge of her nose and slugged her bag onto her shoulder. She turned and walked through the snow to their dorms.

What had Jillian done to provoke this attack? As a friend, shouldn't Cathy be happy that he might have found someone? "Are you okay?" He was concerned by the force with which the snow had hit her.

Rubbing the side of her eye, Jillian tried to play it off. "I take it she doesn't like me."

Worriedly, he reached up to her face. "Are you sure you're all right?"

"I'll be fine. Stop worrying. That's Tara's department."

Tara had come running over to check things out. She snorted in disgust and knelt in front of Jillian. "Bitch!" Tara yelled to the retreating Cathy.

David helped Jillian to her feet "Let me walk you to your room."

Sighing, Jillian responded, "I'm fine. Now stop all this worrying. It'll take a little more than a snowball to get me down."

He walked her to her dorm hoping she really was okay.

After he kissed her outside the building he said, "How about I come by later on to make sure you're really 'fine.'"

A smile began to spread across her lips. "David, seriously, if I were you, I'd be careful. You sound like you might care, and that would break your rule about not—"

He silenced her by putting his index finger to her soft lips. "Aren't rules meant to be broken?"

****

David was more than irritated when he pounded on Cathy's door. "I know you're in there," he shouted.

Casually, as though nothing had occurred earlier, she opened the door to lean against the frame. "David. What a pleasant surprise. Please come in."

He immediately demanded, "Why? Why'd you do that?"

She pushed the hair behind her ears. "Why? Can't I take part in your snowball fight? I didn't know it was a private game."

"Yeah, right." He walked into the middle of the room, and Cathy closed the door.

He continued, "You did that on purpose. You meant to hurt her."

"I don't know what you are talking about." She took off her glasses to wipe an improbable smudge.

"You do know what I am talking about."

Cathy pushed her lips out. In a baby voice, she said, "Oh, did someone's pretty face get hurt?"

Too angry to speak, he folded his arms across his chest.

Lowering her eyelids, she looked up at him, "You're right, David. I meant to hurt her—the same way she's hurt me, by trying to monopolize all your time. She's getting in the way of our friendship."

Cathy placed her hand on his chest, "She's just like

my mother and sister. She uses her looks to get what she wants from men. She doesn't really care about them. It's a game of conquer-and-destroy before moving on to her next victim."

His eyes narrowed. He forcefully removed her hand. "What are you talking about?"

Putting her hands on her hips, she retorted, "Can't you see she's using you? I'm trying to prevent that from happening. You just watch. One day, she'll drop you and just walk away. You won't even see it coming."

Cathy stepped closer, their bodies touching. "When that happens, you need to remember that I'll always be there for you, David. Why can't you give in and accept that we're meant to be together." She forcibly kissed him.

He pushed her away. "You know what you are? You're a beautiful rose. But you have many thorns that hurt and prick those around you."

He started to leave but turned to look at her. "I am warning you, Cathy. Don't even try to come between us."

He left, slamming the door shut, and headed over to Jillian's dorm.

Chapter 8

The campus was quiet on the last day of final exams. Most of the students had already left for break.

Walking through the parking lot next to Jillian's dorm, David paused for a moment and wondered what he was doing. Ever since his blowup with Cathy, he'd been having doubts about Jillian. He considered how much time she spent with other guys, one in particular. Was she just using him, like Cathy had said?

After a long week of exams and working at the hospital, he was tired. But he had to find out what the story was with Jillian. Since there was no attendant at the front desk, he walked up the stairs to her floor contemplating what he would say.

When he knocked, he heard Tara yell, "The door's unlocked."

As soon as he opened it, Tara jumped. She was wearing only jeans and a bra.

He quickly looked away until she was more dressed. "Expecting someone else?"

"Of course. Did you think I was trying to make a move on you?" She pulled a striped sweater over her head. "Okay, I'm clothed. What's up?"

"I came to see Jillian. But since you are here, can I ask you something?"

"Depends," Tara said coyly.

"Is this a game to her?"

Tara's face paled from the question. She reached under the bed to pull out a duffel bag for her clothes. She wouldn't look at him.

He sat on Jillian's bed, patiently waiting for an answer. He needed to know before the break.

Finally, she said, "What are you talking about?"

"A game…to see how many men she can have before she graduates?"

Tara whipped around to look at David. Her normally friendly face looked anything but. "Apparently, you don't know her so well, do you?"

"She's always around other guys. She seems very friendly with a certain one."

Laughing, Tara slapped her hand to her forehead. "You must be referring to Josh. He's very good-looking but would be more attracted to you than to Jillian. If you get my drift."

She continued after he nodded. "Jillian is the kindest, most caring person I've ever met. While she may appear outgoing, she keeps certain things very close, and they have to be pulled from her. She's not like me. I spill my guts all the time. I love her to death, but she's very wary. Probably why she's never really been with a guy, if you know what I mean."

David found this hard to believe. "Okay, then, why me?" he asked skeptically.

Tara started pulling more clothes from her closet to place into the bag on the bed. "Now there's a good question. I've been asking myself the same thing. For the life of me, I can't figure it out. Maybe because you're not falling all over her, like your friend with the curly hair…I can't remember his name."

"Dan?"

"That's it!" She reached under her bed to get out another bag to put the neatly folded clothes in.

Before he could comment further, Tara was facing him with hands on her hips. "I have one thing to say to you. If you don't want to see her because you're torn between her and Cathy, then be truthful and tell her. Don't make up some big lie to spare her feelings. She'll see through it. If you hurt her, then I'll hurt you. Got it?"

"Yes," he answered.

"Good." She continued packing her clothes.

"Cathy is just a friend. Believe me, there is nothing happening there."

"Then you need to tell her that."

"I already did."

"Yeah like that did any good. Either that, or she doesn't care."

Before he could say more, Jillian came into the room. Her face lit up with a smile when she saw him.

Picking up the various bags and tossing them over her shoulder like a bellhop, Tara excused herself. "I'll be waiting downstairs in the car," she told Jillian.

David remained sitting on the bed as Jillian quickly walked toward him. Her shaken-off coat landed on the floor. With her long, lean legs, she straddled him. Her green eyes twinkled as she looked into his. She slid her soft hand over his face and fervently kissed him. He wanted her like he had never wanted anyone before.

Now that he'd heard the truth from her best friend, he let his heart take over.

He cupped her bottom in his hands and pulled her closer. His tongue pushed her mouth open and explored. His hands moved under her sweater and ran up her sides, his thumbs brushing alongside her breasts. He felt her shiver.

Though he'd just found out she was a virgin, she was giving signals that she wanted him physically. His fingertips brushed the thin material of her bra. He could not separate his mouth from hers. His fingers teased her through the lacy material until her nipples were erect. Her breathing became very rapid and a moan escaped her lips.

He lifted the sweater over her head. "Are you all right?"

The look in her eyes said it all. "I'm just tingling all over. That's never happened before," she said before biting her lip.

David stared at her, not certain he'd heard her right. She pressed her lips back to his and ran her fingers through his hair. His lips traced a line down her neck. She leaned her chest into him and tilted her head back. He felt her heart beating. He pushed the flimsy fabric of her bra aside, exposing her breast.

At that moment, there was a knock at the door. "Can I come in?" Tara asked.

The mood was broken.

"Gimme a minute," Jillian stammered. Her face was flushed and her lips swollen.

In a flash, she jumped off his lap, put on her sweater, and checked herself in the mirror.

He came up behind her and put his hands on her shoulders.

She turned to face him. "Can I see you over break?"

"Why do you think I was here waiting for you? I need your phone number."

She found a piece of paper on her desk, scribbled the number, and handed it to him.

When Jillian opened the door, Tara was sitting cross-legged on the floor flipping through a magazine. She had a knowing smile on her face. "It was getting cold sitting in the car. You need to get one with a more reliable heater."

Jillian smirked and rolled her eyes, saying nothing.

David grabbed Jillian's bags and headed to her red Volkswagen. He kissed her goodbye through the rolled-down window.

Chapter 9

Jillian looked up every time she heard the doorbell ring. *Where was he?* David said he was coming for Christmas dinner. Her house was filled with her family and neighbors. She wished Tara was here to help calm her nervous energy, but she had left yesterday to spend a couple of days at her own mother's house.

She knew Nana was watching her every move. Jillian believed that she and Grandpa had been listening in on just about every phone conversation she'd had with David since their arrival. She wouldn't be surprised to find Nana had bugged her phone. Tonight, after everyone left, she'd personally inspect it.

Every time he'd called on the phone, some member of her family found an excuse to be in the room. Hiding in the closet wasn't even an option, because someone would need to get their coat at that exact moment. Jillian couldn't figure why this was happening to her.

Shaking her head in frustration, she went into the kitchen to get some more plates. "Why's everyone so surprised that I have a boyfriend? And why all the sudden interest in my dating life?"

"Because you never really had either one, dear," Nana said.

Not realizing she had spoken these words aloud nor that her grandmother was right behind her, she turned so fast, she nearly dropped the plates.

Nana's green eyes twinkled when she spoke, "It's nothing to be ashamed of, dear. It's just that we're happy you've finally taken an interest in someone, and a doctor to boot. So tell me, are you happy with him?"

"Nana, it's too new to tell. But when I'm with him, I feel like I'm on top of the world." She sighed. "I just hope you like him. He's quiet."

Nana patted her hand, "If you like him and he treats you well, I'll like him."

When the doorbell rang, Jillian looked at Nana. "That's him, I know it." She started to run through the house toward the front door, but Barb beat her there.

"Hello," Barb said hesitantly.

"Mrs. O'Malley?"

"Yes, and you must be David."

"Yes ma'am, I am," he responded. "Sorry, I'm late. Had some car troubles."

Barb opened the door all the way to let him and a large floral holiday arrangement inside. "It's okay. We were just putting out the food."

David handed Barb the flowers.

Standing next to Jillian, Nana whispered, "He sure is a looker. Too bad your grandfather is here, or I'd flirt with him myself. Now introduce me to him."

Jillian chuckled inwardly as she led Nana to David. "Hey, I didn't think you were going to make it." She leaned to give him a peck on the cheek, ignoring the loud sigh coming from Nana.

"David, this is the one-and-only Nana. She's married, and my grandfather is here, so please try not to make a move on her. It could get ugly."

Offended, Barb exclaimed, "Jillian!"

Nana cut her off, "Barb, she's fine. In fact, I'd be

flattered if David flirted with me." Snapping her fingers, she added, "Means I still got it."

Jillian winked at David who chuckled over what he would soon find was Nana's very typical behavior. She took his coat to hang it on the rack in the tiny foyer.

"Come on. I'll introduce you to the rest of the family." Jillian took his hand and led him to the living room where cousins, aunts, and uncles were each trying to be heard over the Christmas music and each other.

When Jillian started introductions, her family practically fell over themselves to meet David. Her grandfather shook his hand so hard, she was positive David's shoulder was dislocated. Her father's sister-in-law, Aunt Donna, who had been drinking the punch ever since she arrived, stumbled over her own feet trying to get off the chair she was lounging in.

The worst was her year-older-than-Jillian cousin Nikki giving him a hug that was a little too long and friendly. Jillian exhaled completely before tapping Nikki's shoulder, signaling time to unwrap herself from his body. Nana looked like she wanted to slap the girl.

"Sorry about that," Jillian whispered to David, guiding him away from her cousin. "Nikki has always been too friendly. She makes Tara look nun-like."

She stopped talking when her dad walked up to them.

Though Jillian was as tall as her father and had inherited his and Nana's bright green eyes, the resemblance ended there. Her jet-black hair, high cheekbones, and warm skin tone was contrasted by his dull red hair and very pale skin that would burn if he was in the sun for more than a few minutes.

"Mr. O'Malley." David extended his hand.

"Ah, David. Please, call me Patrick," he said, shaking the stretched-out hand. "Welcome, and Merry Christmas."

"Thank you, sir."

"Hope you're hungry. We have more food than people. What do you drink? Wine? Beer? Punch?" Her father glanced Jillian's way to signal her to get drinks while he guided David to the dining room where there really was enough food to feed most of their campus.

Rolling her eyes to the ceiling, she realized any wishing for time alone with David had ended. He was engulfed in the O'Malley clutches. If she was lucky, she might have a chance to see him before the night was over.

Leaving the room, she turned to see Nana. "I like him, Jillian. I can feel it."

All she could do was shake her head as she went to bring back drinks. When she returned with three beers, David and her dad were sitting with her Uncle Bob discussing UK's basketball team. Nikki had grabbed the empty chair next to David. It was hopeless. Nikki would not be moved from her perch.

It appeared her family was enthralled with him. Thank goodness!

****

With the exception of her father's snoring in the family room, the house was quiet. The last guest left an hour ago.

David and Jillian sat on the living room couch. The outside Christmas lights were still lit.

"I like your family," he said.

"So they didn't scare you off?" She tucked her legs beneath her. A part of her dreaded his answer—Aunt

Donna and Nikki could be embarrassing. *Maybe* that was why she hadn't dated anyone seriously—fear of how her extended family's actions.

"Well, Nikki did make a profound effort, didn't she?" David smiled at her in the glow of the lights coming from outside. "But overall, I had a good time. Thanks for having me." He started to move as if to get up.

"You're leaving?"

"Do you want me to?"

She pulled on his arm to hold him down. "No. Not yet."

She snickered when a backfiring car-sounding snore came from the next room. "I think after tonight, you'll never look at me the same."

He put his arm around her shoulder and pulled her close to him. "Yours is probably the same as most families out there. I'll admit it, I'm jealous. It wasn't like this for me growing up."

She scrunched her nose at him. "Really? What was your family like? I mean, you never talk about them."

He touched his finger to her nose. "Don't do that. You'll get wrinkles."

She tossed her head and tried to roll her eyes. *How many times had she heard that?*

"Seriously, David. Were they okay with you not seeing them for Christmas?"

"They probably didn't do anything to celebrate. And if I was there, my father would have been complaining about having to buy extra food."

"What? Complain about having family on the holidays?" she said.

"Jillian, I grew up very poor in eastern Kentucky.

We lived in a rundown trailer on the town outskirts that should've been condemned long before we moved in there. My father was an alcoholic who could never hold onto a job. Every time he was fired, he would get meaner and drink even more. My mom had to support us. We barely had enough to eat, and Dad always got first dibs."

"I'm sorry."

David faced her. He took both of her hands in his. "Don't be. The main reason I don't go home is my father can't stand the sight of me."

"What?"

"When I was sixteen, my younger brother Todd cut himself on a fishhook. Neither of us thought anything about it. I told him to rinse his hand in the pond water and then wrap an old cloth around it. Several days went by. His cut was not getting any better, and now he had a fever. We were too poor to take him to the doctor. Todd had always been painfully thin and malnourished. He couldn't fight off the infection and died a week later."

"David, I am so sorry." Jillian looked into his sad, blue eyes. She didn't know what to do to ease his obvious pain.

"My father blamed me for it. Told me it was all my fault. Of course, he failed to recognize that he was the one who wouldn't take Todd to the doctor because he didn't want to tap into his whiskey fund. He told me I had killed his favorite son and I was worthless. The next two years I only slept in the trailer. I spent the rest of my time at school or in the library. The day after I graduated, the old man told me to get out. I haven't been back since."

"What about your mom?" Jillian asked. "Don't you

miss her?"

"I do. Every Mother's Day I drive out and meet her for brunch at the diner before she has to work. I don't understand why she stays with him."

"Maybe, in her own way, she still loves him." Jillian squeezed his hand. "Love makes people do strange things."

"I guess," he said, shrugging. "I hope you now understand why I'm working all the time. I'm entirely self-supported. And when you talk about family, I don't really know what that's about."

She let go of his hand and cupped David's face. "I don't want you to feel I'm demanding anything from you. And I'll share my family with you, if you want." Jillian leaned in to kiss his lips and felt the yearning. Scooting forward, she wrapped her arms around his neck to deepen the kiss.

"Wait," he said, pulling back. "I have something for you."

He stood and walked quickly outside to his Jeep. From the rear of the truck, he pulled a Red Ryder sleigh with a big bow on it. He came up the front porch steps, grinning ear to ear.

"I thought this might be more comfortable than those cafeteria trays."

She held her hands over her mouth. It was a simple gift, but it was the best one she'd received all day. She remembered how it felt to be sledding on his lap. In that brief second, she had known he would protect her from anything.

She kissed him. She was stalling, because suddenly her gift was all wrong for him. But he'd think she hadn't thought of him at all if she didn't give it to him.

She walked slowly up the stairs, "Wait right here," she whispered.

Coming back down the stairs with two large, wrapped boxes, she reluctantly said, "These are for you."

David sat back down on the couch to unwrap the boxes, handing her the discarded paper. Inside the first was a leather jacket.

Every time Jillian had seen him in his coat, she wondered how old it was and how long he'd had it.

Inside the other box were several heavy cotton button-down shirts. "Are you trying to tell me something, Jillian?" he asked.

Biting her lip, she wasn't sure if he was teasing. She realized there was nothing to say that wouldn't offend or hurt his feelings if she said how old and worn some of his clothes looked.

He cupped her chin in his hands to turn her face to his. "I know I've needed a new coat for a while, but shopping just seems a bother. If I had a choice between buying new clothes and spending time with you, I think you know what I chose."

He touched his lips to hers. "You," he said between his feathered kisses.

Chapter 10

They had been dating for a month, and the sexual tension between them was high. David knew Jillian was a virgin so didn't want to push her. On the other hand, he had seen enough photos of her to know she could easily put on a seductive look. He wondered if she really wanted to be with him.

Tara needed to borrow her car, so he had agreed to drive Jillian to Louisville for a photo shoot that afternoon. He opted to sit and study in the nearby coffee shop while she worked. After several hours, he decided to head back to the studio to see if she was done yet. Really, how much time was needed to take a few pictures?

An overly-thin girl, wearing too much makeup to his liking, brought him to where Jillian was. Over the loud music, voices shouted out orders. It amazed him anyone could hear anything other than Prince singing.

With the crowd of people surrounding the bright lights, he heard her before he saw her.

"I am smiling! Maybe if you took the lens cover off, you'd see that."

Her words stunned him. Usually she was so quiet and reserved. He immediately got the feeling that when pushed, she would easily fight back. *Good for her.*

An older, pudgy man standing to the side with his arms crossed said, "I think we should take a five-minute break. Give everyone a chance to calm down."

The ponytailed cameraman looked toward the older man and shrugged his shoulders in disgust.

"It's your dollar," he said. "But I'm not ready to take a break." He pointed to Jillian and continued, "If she would cooperate a little, we'd be done in no time at all."

When the cameraman moved to the side, David saw Jillian. She was lying on her side, in a black cocktail dress, on a table covered with satiny white cloth. Her left arm supported her head with her hair pulled loosely on top. Around her neck was a large emerald pendant. Matching earrings dangled from her ears. This was not the same girl who a few hours earlier walked away from him in sweat pants, an oversized UK sweatshirt, and baseball cap.

One of the men working the lights turned to Jillian and in a loud whisper said, "Jilly, pretend that guy you were telling me about earlier is here. That will put you in the mood."

She closed her eyes for what seemed like minutes, and David watched a slight smile pass over her lips. When she opened her eyes, they locked onto his. Not only did he witness the transformation, but so did everyone else in the studio. She looked almost sultry. And it was because of him.

The photographer fervently snapped pictures, talking while moving about. David didn't hear the words being said. The sound of his heart beating for her drowned everything else out.

"Jilly, perfect. Keep thinking of him." The photographer stepped in front of David. When Jillian moved her head to see David better, the cameraman stopped and slowly turned to find what was capturing her attention. Immediately he looked back to Jillian, and then again to David.

Raising his eyebrow high, he said, "See? You wished so hard that you actually made him appear. Pretty amazing, love!"

The photographer snapped his fingers at two women standing by the older gentleman. He pointed to Jillian. One rushed forward to change the jewelry, and the other loosened Jillian's hair from its clip. A third touched up her makeup.

Jillian broke in, "Marco, that's David. The guy I was telling you about."

Marco nodded his chin in acknowledgement before turning his camera back to Jillian. He positioned her to lean against the back of a chair. "Maybe he should come along more often. Then I wouldn't have to lose my temper with you."

Jillian shook her head at his words. The session was soon over.

Before they departed, the older, heavy gentleman came over to introduce himself as Joe Hannaford, owner of the jewelry store. "Mr. Rainier, when you see these ads, you should remember that Jillian's mysterious look was meant for you and you only."

Those words stayed with David on their hour-long drive back to Lexington. Every so often he would steal a glance at Jillian while she chatted. She would stop and give him that same look she'd given at the studio. He wanted her now.

When he pulled his Jeep to a stop in front of the resident apartments, he leaned over to kiss her. "Come upstairs with me," he whispered in her ear.

She nodded, and the two raced up the stairs to the living quarters he shared with Eric, Dan, and another medical student she'd not yet met.

David didn't acknowledge anyone passing in the hall. He seemed to take forever to unlock the door. They wordlessly hurried into his room. Once inside, with the door closed, they threw their knapsacks to the floor. He took Jillian in his arms and held her close, covering her with kisses.

He guided her to his bed. Her swollen, full lips were slightly parted. Her eyes were waiting. She touched his face with light fingers. He lifted her sweatshirt over her head.

He debated on slowing the pace but decided against it when her hands wrapped around his neck pulling him to her. He tasted her sweetness and knew this was it. She wrapped her legs around his waist, pressing herself to him. He adjusted himself on top of her. She moaned, feeling how much he wanted her.

The sound of someone's throat clearing was followed by the words, "This is a surprise. I thought we were getting together to study for our exam tomorrow."

David snapped his head up to see Cathy, arms crossed, standing in the doorway.

An exclamation of surprise escaped Jillian when she saw Cathy glaring at them.

David rolled off Jillian, using her body to hide his shrinking erection. Jillian lifted one knee a little bit to help him out. He kept his arm draped over her middle, hoping Cathy would get the hint, especially since Jillian was only wearing a lacy bra and sweatpants. Annoyed, he asked, "What are you doing here?"

"Dan and I heard voices when we came into the

apartment. Silly me, I thought we'd study together, like *we always* do."

Jillian's body tensed next to his. Shaking his head in disgust, he replied, "Haven't you heard of privacy?"

Sarcastically, Cathy sighed. "Hey, if you want privacy, I suggest you lock the door next time." She stormed from the room, leaving the door open.

Jillian sat straight up in bed. "Man, does she know how to shatter a moment, or what? I'll go, so you can study and not be distracted."

He reached out for her hand. "Stay here. I want you to."

"The mood's over. Glasses ruined it. I'm going back to my room to watch *Moonlighting* with Tara."

"Watch it here. You won't bother me."

He watched as she internally wrestled with a decision. He got off the bed to pick up his book bag from the floor.

She put her top back on and made herself comfortable on his bed to watch TV. Before the show ended, she was under his covers fast asleep.

From his desk, he watched her, wanting to feel her body next to his.

****

Jillian awoke with a start knowing she was in a strange place. She looked around and saw David sleeping on the bed on the other side of the room. She rubbed her eyes trying to focus on the alarm clock on the desk. Six o'clock.

She lay completely still. She had spent the night fully-clothed in David's room while he slept in another bed. Okay, what did that say? Was he trying to be a gentleman? Why? She wanted him and thought he wanted her just as much.

She rubbed her hand through her hair ordering herself to stop analyzing this and think clearly.

Jillian looked back at him. He looked peaceful. His chest rose with each deep breath. More than anything, what she wanted was to walk over to him, touch the hard angles of his face, and lay beside him.

Slowly and quietly, she slipped out of bed and practically fell, tripping over her shoes lying haphazardly on the floor. She could never be a spy. Picking up her shoes, she tiptoed over to her bag. Very slowly, in order not to make a sound, she turned the door handle. She leaned over to put on her shoes and hurried down the hall, hoping not to see anyone.

The stairwell, where she planned to make her escape, was located across the hall from the elevators. She heard the elevator's bell that dinged before its doors opened. She held her breath and swiftly rushed into the stairwell. As the door was closing, Jillian peered through the crack and saw Cathy inside the conveyance reading a newspaper. When the elevator shut, Jillian started breathing again. She hoped Cathy hadn't seen her.

****

Slowly, Jillian walked to the housing complex where Eric and David lived. She was glad this week—possibly the longest one of her life—was over. She had spent every evening in the library finishing her history paper and studying for mid-term exams, all while student teaching.

At least being busy kept her mind from reliving the night in David's room. Crossing the street now, she told herself to stop thinking about it and concentrate on something else—like what she was going to pack for the Cancun spring break trip with Tara and Josh.

Near the housing complex, she heard someone calling her name. Turning around, she was shocked to see Glasses.

Cathy asked, "Are you here to see David?"

Jillian nodded and tucked a piece of hair behind her ears. What was with this sudden interest and seeming friendliness Cathy was exhibiting?

"Do you mind, if I walk with you, then?" Cathy asked innocuously.

Jillian shrugged her shoulders

"Has David told you where he's planning on doing his residency? He and I applied to go to the same places, and I already received my letter. I'm heading to Atlanta. I think he is, too."

Jillian gave Cathy a questioning look. She couldn't believe what she had just heard. "Where else had he applied?" She hoped her voice wouldn't give away her hurt feelings.

Cathy quickly replied, "Nowhere around here, of course. Only Eric wants to stay nearby. David and I applied to hospitals in Atlanta, Philadelphia, Charlotte, and Denver. Didn't he tell you?"

"No." Jillian stuffed her shaking hands in her jean pockets, willing herself to be calm.

Stopping short, Cathy put her hand over her mouth as if in shock. "Uh-oh. Jillian, I'm sorry I said anything. I truly am. You know how he can be. He probably didn't share since he knew things with you would be short-lived."

"Short-lived?"

"Yes. He doesn't want to stay around here. He's

said he's 'off to bigger things.' This is what he's been dreaming of."

Jillian regarded Cathy before starting to walk to her original destination. Trying to sound unshaken, she asked, "Why are you suddenly sharing with me when you've made it clear you don't even like me?"

Cathy looked Jillian directly in the eye. In a sincere-sounding tone she replied, "The fact is we're both attracted to him. But he doesn't belong to either of us. I have the advantage of having his friendship for years. I know things about him that you don't. In all that time, I've learned he doesn't get close to anyone who may get in the way of achieving his goals. He's told me many times that he has no plans for a long-term relationship. It would only hold him back."

She was speechless as the words sank in. She searched Cathy's face for any sign of malicious intent. It was hard to tell. The face behind those awful glasses was always stern and void of any emotion.

Jillian took a deep breath of spring air. Putting on an exaggerated smile, she said, "Thanks for telling me. At least now I'll be prepared when he breaks the news." She continued to walk toward the building with Cathy at her side.

They climbed the stairs in silence. When Jillian exited on David's floor, Cathy didn't acknowledge her departure. She kept walking until she was outside David's door. She wasn't sure how long she stood there. Her mind was in turmoil. She remembered Eric saying he was happy he was doing his residency in Lexington. *He must know, too,* she thought. Why hadn't he told her? She reasoned that it was probably because everyone was aware it was *temporary* with her.

She turned around and headed back down the stairs to return to her dorm.

In her room, she tugged off her jeans and put on a pair of pajama pants. After climbing into her bed, she yanked the covers over her head and closed her eyes. *Everything always happens for a reason,* she thought.

She woke when Tara came into the room, sat on her bed, and asked, "Are you okay?"

Jillian opened her eyes. "No," she cried. "He's leaving. He didn't have the nerve to tell me. He's going with Cathy to some place out of state. And to think I was falling for him. I thought he cared for me, but he tells Cathy all the important news in his life. Not me! He looks at me as a temporary fling." She couldn't say any more, her voice was choking with tears.

"What are you talking about?"

Jillian sniffled a few times and blew her nose. "His residency. He's going to Atlanta with Glasses. And he's looking at me as a short-term thing. And I had to hear this from Cathy because he apparently doesn't want to tell me." The tears started again.

"I think you're jumping to conclusions." Tara stood up to find more tissues. "If it was me, I wouldn't trust anything Glasses says. I bet she's making the whole thing up to get in between you two. Let me do some investigating. I was just over there, and so was he."

"No, don't bother. I think I'm going to pack and head home.

"No, you are not," Tara ordered, picking up her keys. "We're going to get to the bottom of this. Now let's head over so we can find out."

"Not tonight. Maybe tomorrow. I just want to be

alone right now."

"Fine, have it your way, but I bet this is one big misunderstanding. When I find out, remind me that I was right. Tootles."

After Tara left, Jillian lay on the bed for some time before getting up to pack her clothes. After she had everything in her bag, she went down to Josh's room to see what he was doing. When her knocks went unanswered, she went back to her room. There she found Tara waiting with two cartons of ice cream.

"Here, I got you this from Graeter's. I think you're going to need it."

Jillian took the carton. She looked out the window to see the sun setting. "I take it you were not right."

"I guess not. You should count yourself lucky to have a friend like me."

"Oh no! What have you done?" Jillian asked, turning around.

"Calm down. I was just looking out for you. When I arrived, David was there. I think he thought it was you when I knocked. As soon as he opened the door, I casually asked him if he had heard where he was doing his residency. When he said 'yes,' I hauled off and punched him. I told him 'that's what you get for hurting Jillian.' I turned around and stormed down the hall."

Tara stopped talking long enough to scoop out a big spoon of chocolate ice cream.

"You did what?"

"You heard me. Well Eric followed me out, and when I gave him the details, he shook his head in disbelief. He told me all he knows is David wanted to tell you first, and that he doesn't even know where David is going. When I asked, he said that, in the past,

David had said he wasn't into having a serious relationship. I told him I thought it was best if David gave you some space for a few days and that maybe you two could talk after spring break."

Jillian didn't say anything. She could not get the image of Tara hitting David from her mind.

"Your bags are packed, right?" Tara asked. "I think we should spend the night at Nana's. Your parents will ask too many questions."

"Wait," Jillian said. "Don't you have a date tonight?"

"Yes, but I can cancel."

"No, go out. I'll go to Nana's for the night and will be back tomorrow loaded with her cooking."

"Are you sure?"

"Yes." Jillian picked up the tub of ice cream and carried it to the refrigerator. Looking out the window, she saw a solitary figure pacing in front of her dorm. She knew it was David and immediately backed away from the window.

She couldn't talk with him right now. She needed a night to clear her head and brace herself for the news. She picked up her overnight bag, walked down the hall, and slipped out the side door to her car.

Chapter 11

Nana opened the door as soon as her car turned into the driveway. Jillian walked into the open arms of the woman who was always there for her.

After Jillian shared the day's events, Nana patted her arm. "You know, this could all be a big mix-up. You need to talk to David. He might he hurting, too."

"I will. I just can't do it tonight, or even tomorrow."

Nana shook her head and looked Jillian squarely in the eye. "You are *so* stubborn. You must have gotten that from your mother's side of the family because we know I'm very easy-going."

Jillian sighed.

Nana continued, "When you talk with him, listen patiently to what he has to say. Don't jump to conclusions, as you are now."

They sat together in the keeping room off the kitchen. Jillian rocked in her favorite chair. "I don't know what to do, Nana."

Nana lifted a finger and pointed it at Jillian's heart. Softly she said, "Yes, you do. The answer is inside there. You're leaving on your trip in a week. Do you want this heavy feeling hanging over you that whole time?"

"No."

"Listen to me, because I won't say it again. Tell

David how you feel. If he doesn't listen, then I was wrong…for the first time in my life. Don't throw away a good thing, Jillian. Life's too short and precious."

Nana gazed outside. "When you're young, you think you've got all the time in the world. Then, one morning, you wake up and there is an old face, lined with wrinkles and gray hair, looking back at you from the mirror. You not only wonder who that face belongs to, but where the time went."

****

The next day after lunch Jillian hugged Nana goodbye. Visiting her grandmother was therapeutic. She made everything better.

Driving to campus with the windows down, she sang all the songs on the radio.

She parked her car in the parking lot across from David's dorm. She sat for a long time, summoning the courage to walk inside. "What am I scared of?" she asked herself. "I already know what the worst thing he can say is."

Jillian closed her eyes and breathed in deeply before opening her car door. Slowly, she walked to the front door. Suddenly her legs stopped moving, and she stood on the bottom stair looking at the door leading into his building. Her legs felt wobbly, and she sat on the step. She couldn't make herself go in.

Biting her bottom lip, she thought about the various possibilities. She could stay here until he either came out or went inside. However, that could be hours. She was a wimp, definitely not a fighter.

She didn't have to wait hours. Eric and Tara came out of the building, laughing. Their laughter ceased when they saw her.

They sat down on either side of the silent Jillian. She glanced at both of them. "What've you two been up to?" she asked, knowing what their answer was.

Tara responded lightly, "We saw your car in the parking lot and came down to see you."

Eric put his hand on her knee and said, "The two of you really need to talk. He's been intolerable."

Jillian ran her fingers through her long hair.

Eric continued, "If you want my opinion, you two belong together. It's obvious how much you care for each other. Plus, he needs you. Ever since he met you, he's been a completely different person. He actually sees there's more to life than school."

Still biting her lip, Jillian looked over at Eric's caring eyes.

Tara leaned over to give her a hug. She whispered softly in her ear, "Be strong and listen to him. Don't chicken out on me." She pulled away and looked straight into Jillian's eyes. "I want you to know, I apologized to him for what I did."

Sitting up straighter, she gave Tara a questioning look.

Eric jumped up. "He should be getting off work about now. Why don't you wait upstairs?"

She nodded, still taken aback by Tara's words.

"Come on then, I'll let you in," Eric said.

The three walked in silence to the apartment. Several residents had given the trio an odd look. Everyone must have heard what Tara had done.

Jillian threw her purse on the bed and walked around Eric and David's cramped bedroom. She stopped in front of Eric's desk. It was cluttered with pictures of him with family and friends. Books were open. Some pages had doodles on them.

David' desk, which faced the window, was bare except for a few books and a penholder. The only personal item was a picture of the two of them from New Year's Eve. She thought, *he must have an easy time packing.* She looked out the window onto the green.

Glancing at the clock, she finally sat on his bed. He should've been back by now. She had too much nervous energy to sit quietly and immediately stood up to walk to the window again. She hugged her arms together. She could feel herself getting more edgy. What was she going to say? She wouldn't say anything. *He'll do the talking, I'll listen.*

She didn't hear the key turn in the lock but about-faced when the main door squeaked open. She walked to the bedroom's open doorway. Her hand flew to cover her mouth. Jillian took a few steps back when she saw the bruise next to his eye. *Ouch!* Tara was small, but forceful.

David came into the bedroom. Turning his back on her, he silently closed the door. He was obviously surprised to see her. Still facing the door, he shook his head and said very seriously, "We need to talk."

Jillian swallowed hard and closed her eyes. She knew what was coming. She kept repeating to herself *be strong. Pretend you're on a photo shoot, and they are barking out orders.*

When he turned to face her there was no emotion in his face. "Do you want to sit?" he asked.

She nodded her head. She didn't trust her legs to not fail and give out. She pulled the wooden chair from his desk and sat, leaning her side against its back for support.

David sat on the edge of Eric's desk. The silence in the room was unbearable. "I wanted to tell you where I was going for my residency. I wanted to see the look on your face when you found out...*from me*. I had the whole night planned." He looked at the floor. "Best laid plans gone awry."

"Where are you going?" Jillian was genuinely surprised her voice did not shake when she asked. She moved her hands beneath her on the chair. She was trembling.

He stared at her. She saw the pain in his eyes, and it tore at her. "I'm petitioning to stay here." There was a long pause before he finally whispered, "To be with you."

She hadn't realized she had been holding her breath until she felt it all escaping her body. She hadn't expected this. He wasn't leaving her after all!

She didn't know what to say or do. Tears ran from her eyes. She bit her lip. She started to rise from the chair to tell him she was sorry, but the look on his face stopped her.

His voice was too quiet when he whispered, "Why? Why did you believe what Cathy said? You know how she is. Why didn't you come talk to me?"

Jillian sat, not knowing what to say. What he said was true. A part of her had not trusted Cathy, and yet she had still believed her.

"Why? Because...she's always with you. Because of the things she said." To Jillian's own ears, this wasn't making sense. Finally, she gave up, looked at the floor, and said, "I don't know."

His shoulders slumped. "I had to hear it from Tara.

When I got up to your room, I found out you'd left minutes earlier." He stopped and looked toward the window.

Jillian reminded herself to keep her mouth shut so she didn't say the wrong thing.

"You know what hurts the most? That you didn't trust me. Did you honestly think I was going to just up and walk away like that? Do you think that I don't care about you?"

She shook her head.

"I debated telling you where I had applied. I was afraid you and I wouldn't have made it this long. You see, I put myself in your shoes. If I thought *you* were leaving, I'm not sure I would have made a commitment to be with you. Honestly, I could see you thinking of it as a fling, with no emotions attached. But I couldn't do that to us."

Jillian swallowed hard again. "I'm sorry. I can see now that what I did was wrong. I was hurt and needed time by myself to think and sort it all out. I needed to prepare myself for your leaving."

The stillness hung in the room. Neither said anything.

David finally continued, "I'm not leaving you, Jillian."

She tried to smile. When her bottom lip began to quiver, she bit hard on it. "I'm glad to hear that. Because even with all the thinking I did last night, I couldn't really prepare myself to hear you say goodbye."

He came over and squatted in front of her.

She searched his deep blue eyes for any clue of his thoughts. The longer the silence continued, the worse she felt. Jillian caressed the bruised skin around his eye with her thumb. She felt him lean into her hand.

"I'm sorry for what happened, and about what Tara did to you. It's my—"

Taking hold of her hand and looking into her eyes, he interrupted, "I love you, Jillian."

Her heart stopped. Had she heard correctly? Time stopped. Was she even breathing? She couldn't tell. He had just said the words she had hoped to hear. She knocked him over when she fell into his arms.

"I love you, too," she said through her tears. For the first time in her life, she had given her heart away, and it felt right. Nana hadn't been wrong.

Kneeling on the floor together, he kissed her passionately on the lips, eyes, and nose. She ran her arms up his chest and around his neck.

David stood, pulling her up, and led her to the bed where she lay down beside him. He propped himself up on one arm to look at her. His other hand ran along her face and down her neck. His lips trailed the same path. Her breathing became ragged. His fingers ran over the fabric of her blouse, and he began to unbutton it. When all were undone, he stopped.

Jillian was nervous. Seeing the heat in his eyes, she reached behind his neck to pull him to her. She ran her fingers through his hair, massaging his scalp.

His breathing quickened. With one hand, he opened her blouse and began to gently rub her small breasts through a layer of thin lace.

Her chest was rising up and down. Soon, the clasp on the front of her bra had been unfastened exposing her breasts to him. Her skin was wanting to be touched. Excitement rose in her as he circled each mound with his finger making his way to the nipples. His tongue followed.

She squirmed, in a state of euphoria. Her body was aching for him. She was relaxed, nervous, and excited all at the same time. Every hair on her body was standing and tingling. Her girl parts wanted his boy parts. She did not want him to stop this time. She had no control over her body.

When his tongue circled her nipple, she felt a tingle between her legs and a moan escaped her lips. He stopped to look at her. She wanted to feel his skin against hers. She unbuttoned his shirt, and he sat up enough for her to push it off his broad shoulders.

His hard, tight chest had a scattering of dark brown hair, the same color and texture as the hair on his head. She ran her fingers through it. She could feel his muscles react to her touch. She continued to caress his chest before moving her hands over his shoulders and back up to his face. She saw his responses to her touch, and knew their excitement levels matched at this moment.

He moved, and Jillian felt his hardness against her thigh. She returned to running her fingers over his chest. He guided her hand down to the button on his jeans. She obligingly undid them.

She kissed his lips, her tongue exploring his mouth. She wrapped her leg around his hip and pulled him on top of her. Tingling with excitement, she enjoyed the feel of his bare skin against her. She slid her hands down his back and underneath the backside of his jeans. His butt was firm. She heard his heavy breathing in her ears.

He lifted himself from her and removed her jeans.

She was completely naked beneath him. She saw the look of love in his eyes. She sensed he knew he was about to take her virginity from her. Though nervous, she trusted he would be gentle with her.

He whispered into her ear, "I love you, Jillian."

"Then make love to me," she whispered back.

He took off his jeans and boxers and threw them onto the floor. He was incredible to look at. Her apprehension returned when she saw how large and thick he was. He pulled the covers over them. Rolling on his side, he pulled her against him. She could not think of anything else with his nakedness against her. She was aroused with the feel of his hard erection resting on her thigh.

"I'll try not to hurt you. You set the pace. Okay?" He softly caressed her breasts. He lowered his mouth onto hers and ravenously kissed her. His tongue possessively took hers and demanded more.

She licked her lips.

He slowly ran his hand over her flat stomach, moving to the top of her hipbone, then the top of her leg. Her muscles tightened and her breathing changed. He kept his mouth on hers. He slowly moved down her neck and between her breasts. Her body jumped when his hand ran up the inside of her thigh.

He paused, and they stared at one another. "I can stop," he whispered.

She shook her head slowly. "Don't you dare." She was going to explode if he did not touch her where she most wanted him to soon. His fingers spread the folds between her legs. Lordy, how she wanted him. He stroked her inside. She began to groan and raised her hips to him. He continued to make love with his tongue to her breasts.

She thought she was dying. She could not stand it anymore. She ran her fingers through his hair and pulled him back up to her. "Please, David. I want you," she gasped.

He shifted his entire body on top of hers. She spread her legs for him, and he slowly, gently penetrated her. He stopped when he would feel her body tense. She looked at him, wanting him.

He thrust himself inside of her. When she cried out, he covered her mouth with his. He wrapped his arms around her. He went still before pulling back a little, before entering her again.

It hurt, but at the same time she wanted him to continue moving. Once her body relaxed a little, and she could feel him pulsating, she felt a strong surge pass through her. "David," she moaned, feeling his back and forth movement. "Omigawd."

He joined her in the ecstasy that she was feeling. He lay on top of her, both exhausted and damp with sweat. Neither could breathe. They clung to each other.

"I'm sorry," he said, knowing she had experienced some pain.

"You shouldn't be." Jillian smiled, even though she felt some soreness.

David rolled to his side and held her in his arms. They lay in silence, both too spent to move. She wanted time to stop. *This is perfect*, she thought.

Soon, they fell asleep. Waking after midnight, they made love again. She could not ask for a more tender and gentle introduction to the world of intimacy.

In the room's darkness, they discussed her trip for spring break. She laughed and told him that he had nothing to worry about while she was gone. She reminded him she was twenty-one and had just lost her virginity. Jillian reached up and touched his bruise. "Does it still hurt?"

"Not anymore. I did learn my lesson, though."

"And what was that?" she asked, smiling.

"Don't hurt someone Tara is friends with."

She smiled again and kissed him goodnight. They slept on their sides in the narrow bed with her spooned into him. She held his one arm to her chest, close to her heart. She wouldn't let go of him.

Chapter 12

After a week of continuous rain, the sun finally came out for their May graduation. Jillian sat, with other graduates, listening to the commencement speaker discuss their futures. She daydreamed about her own fate after walking across the stage for her degree.

Before David, she and Tara had it all figured out. They would get a small apartment in Lexington, near Tara's job at a small accounting firm. Jillian was to model over the summer before she started teaching in August. That was supposed to have been the plan.

David's petition to stay in the area wasn't approved. He was heading to Knoxville. The only saving grace was Cathy wouldn't be in the same town.

Jillian and David had spent the last several weeks talking about how they could make this work. Of course, he had asked her to come with him, but she reminded him of the year-long contract she signed with the school district. It wouldn't be right to back out.

It was only twelve months they kept telling themselves. She could look into a teaching job in Tennessee for the autumn after. She knew she would want something from him before she made a commitment like that. She feared mentioning the 'M' word. He might run as he'd made it abundantly clear how his focus was on becoming a doctor.

After the ceremony, there was the endless taking of

pictures. She'd been photographed more than enough in her lifetime, but she still put on her signature smile for the cameras.

At her parents' house, where she and Tara would live until their apartment was ready in a few weeks, her relatives had gathered.

"Tara, have you seen David?" Jillian asked when she couldn't find him. Come to think of it, she hadn't seen her cousin Nikki either, though David generally avoided her like the plague. "I checked inside to see if he was watching the game."

"Nope," Tara replied nonchalantly. She was sitting on the glider with her latest boyfriend, Mike. She and Eric had stopped being an item soon after spring break.

"That's weird. I thought he was here with you all. I was just inside for a minute to see if Barb or Nana needed help."

Tara pointed to the nearby folding chair. "Why don't you have a seat? All your up-and-down and running-around is making me tired. Nana and Barb said this party was for us, so stop working it. I'm sure David is fine, wherever he is."

Jillian instinctively knew something was up. Tara was horrible at surprises and keeping secrets. She cocked her head to the side, "What are you hiding?

"Nothing."

Jillian watched David and her father walk into the backyard together. They were talking up a storm while looking at her. Her father had the same smile on his face that he had earlier when she'd walked across the stage with her diploma.

David walked up to her. He immediately put one knee on the ground. Tara had a big grin on her face.

When he took Jillian's hand, she immediately knew what was going on.

"Jillian," David said, "before I met you, I had one purpose in life—to be a doctor. After I met you, I had a second ambition—and that was to spend the rest of my life with you."

She knew she wasn't blinking. Her teeth caught on her bottom lip.

He slipped a solitaire on her left hand. "Will you marry me?"

She nodded her head and squeaked out, "Yes."

Jillian threw her arms around his neck and they kissed passionately in front of an applauding crowd of her family and friends. When she stood on weak knees she was engulfed in hugs from the throng.

She pointed at Tara. "You knew about this, didn't you?"

"Of course. Who do you think helped him pick out the ring at Hannaford Brothers? In fact, Mr. Hannaford remembered David and took care of him personally."

Before either she or Tara could say more, her aunt and uncle were giving her bear hugs.

Her dad finally hugged her. "I hope this is what you want."

"It is," she answered. She knew her father's skepticism was based on her hardly ever, okay never, really dating. "We're not rushing into anything, Dad. We're going to be apart for a whole year while I teach here and he does his residency in Tennessee."

"He's a good person for you, sweetie." Her dad smiled. "Did I ever tell you how proud I am of you?"

Jillian couldn't answer and instead gave him a tearful hug.

She heard his whisper of regrets about his absence from her life when he was at her mom's side battling the breast cancer, and then again while he grieved her passing. He was a good man, and he'd spent the last ten years trying to make up for this.

When she was finally with David again, she looked down at the ring, still amazed at his proposal.

"We'll make it work, Jillian. We have the summer to be together before school starts. Knoxville is only three hours away. You can help me look for an apartment. There're three-day weekends and holiday breaks. Before you know it, a year will have passed."

"You know I have a few modeling jobs this summer, right?" she asked.

"I do, but that won't be the whole time, will it?"

"That's true." She smiled back at him. "We'll just have to talk with Barb and see what she's lined up for me."

"I love you, Jillian."

She leaned into him. "And I love you back."

Chapter 13

Jillian parked in front of David's small one-bedroom apartment unit near the hospital. She carried up a box of things she'd found, trying to make the place more homey for the next year. After they were married, they would have to find a larger place. This place could hardly hold one person.

She opened the door and set the box on the counter—the only eating area, unless you counted sitting on the floor and using the coffee table her parents had donated to the cause as a dining table.

Not much had changed since she was here a few weeks ago. The sterile environment's only disorder was medical books haphazardly stacked by the sofa. In fact, the afghan she had used at school was still folded in the corner.

She set about retrieving the other box from the car before unpacking and placing the items around the room. She set up the new lamp on the table by the sofa, along with coasters—no more using paper towels for that job. There were a few throw pillows for the couch. And then there was the working toaster that didn't smoke if used more than two times in a row.

She decided to use the bottom drawer of David's dresser to stash some of her clothes and carefully moved his neatly-folded clothes into another drawer that appeared to have plenty of room. He would have cringed at either her or Tara's jammed-packed dressers or closets.

As lunchtime approached, Jillian opened the small refrigerator. It was empty save a container of half-and-half, cola, and orange juice. Seriously? She was a model and knew a thing or two about not having unlimited food available, but this was inhumane even by her standards.

Grabbing her keys, she headed for the store to stock up on food. After filling an entire grocery cart with staples, she headed back to David's apartment and pulled in right behind him. She waved when he got out of his Jeep.

"What are you doing here?" He ran a hand through his dark, week-overdue-for-a-cut hair. Add that to the list of things she needed to handle. "I didn't think you were coming for another few days."

She opened the car trunk. "No, I told you I was coming down on Thursday. I think I left you four messages about it," she replied. "Can you come help me carry all this up?"

As he neared, the bags and dark circles under his blue eyes were clearly visible.

"When was the last time you slept?" she asked.

He leaned down and kissed her. "I can't remember. They warned us about the long hours when I entered medical school, but I didn't think it would be like this." He grabbed three of the bags. "You didn't have to buy all this."

"I know, but I wanted to. Plus I can't survive on the nothingness you have in your fridge."

She lifted the remaining bags out to walk with him up the two flights to his place. "Have you talked to Eric or Dan? Are they working the same insane schedule you are?"

"I keeping playing phone tag with Eric, but I talked with Cathy a few times and it's the same for her."

Lovely. Just lovely. Has the time to talk with Cathy, but not me.

He stopped at the apartment's threshold, seeing the changes she'd made. "What did you do?" he asked.

She darted around him to drop the bags on the counter. "Made it more comfy."

"You don't need to spend your money, Jillian. I'm hardly here. Just like you didn't need to buy all this food."

"You are quite welcome. I just thought it would be a cozier place for you to come home to after work. Plus, in case you forgot, I'll be here every once in a while."

"When I come home, I take a shower and fall into bed. I eat at the hospital, too."

"And we know how good that food can be." Jillian glared at him for his ingratitude. "Why don't you go take that shower and go to bed? I can occupy myself."

"Jillian, I didn't mean it that way."

She held up her hand to stop him. "You're tired and cranky. Before either one of us says something we'll later regret, go to bed."

With that she turned her back to unpack the food. She was tired too but knew he wouldn't understand. She had arrived in Lexington yesterday afternoon after spending three weeks on the road for different modeling shots. When she got home, she and Tara sat up until the wee hours of the morning catching up, even though they talked on the phone every few days. They discussed Tara's loathsome job, Jillian's modeling shoots, what color they wanted to paint the living room, and proposed wedding dates. It would have to be in the summer, when school was not in session, so they had a year to plan.

Once Tara left for work, Jillian jumped in the car to make the three-hour drive to Knoxville. Driving the interstate through the mountains, with tractor trailer trucks, was nerve-wracking.

Once everything was put away, she walked quietly to the bedroom where David was already asleep. Opening the bottom drawer, she pulled out her workout clothes. She'd go for a walk and see what was near the apartment that was fun to do.

****

When David finally woke, it was dark outside. He could make out the shape of Jillian's sleeping body on the other side of the bed. The clock told him it was two in the morning. He'd slept for twelve hours. Lying on his back, he stared at the ceiling trying to remember when he had last slept more than four hours in a row.

He knew he'd been abrupt with Jillian. The fatigue, after working twenty straight hours for each of the last few days, was to blame. He reminded himself this was part of becoming a doctor. The rewards in the future would be worth it.

On his drive home, all he could think about was taking a long, hot shower and falling into bed for a few days. The last thing he expected was for Jillian to show up, looking perfect and beautiful while he felt scruffy and unkempt. Jillian with her big, kind heart didn't deserve his insolence. Quietly he slipped from bed and walked to the kitchen in his boxers.

He filled a glass with water before looking in the

fridge to see what she'd bought that was good to eat. There was a salad that would last a few days, along with something that looked like baked ziti with meat. For someone so intent on not gaining weight and eating super-healthy, she could make big meals. Out of one corner of the dish, there looked to be about three small forkfuls missing. Probably her dinner.

Scooping a big portion onto a plate, he put it in the dated counter-top microwave. While he waited, he thought about what he was going to do with Jillian. He loved her, but he hated being treated as if he were a charity that needed financial support. The two times she'd come to visit, she stocked his kitchen and bought things for the apartment. Granted, he didn't have extra cash right now like she had, but he knew his hard work and dedication would pay for them to live a comfortable life.

Besides I'm really not here at the apartment much he reasoned. He came here to sleep, shower, and study his medical journals. He took the warm plate from the microwave. He hadn't even met any of his neighbors.

He took a bite of the delicious pasta, savoring the flavor. *Man, can she cook.* She probably learned from her grandmother. Nana made the best dinners he'd ever had in his life.

Sitting on the sofa to finish eating, he decided not to say anything. It would only hurt her feelings. He would just try to find a way to prevent it from happening again. How? He'd have to think about that. He had tomorrow, or really today, off and would make the effort to spend it with Jillian. She had driven all the way from Lexington to be with him.

After setting the empty plate in the sink, he quietly

crawled back into bed next to her.

****

Later that afternoon David and Jillian walked, holding hands, to the park at the end of his street. "I can't believe you've never noticed it before." Jillian looked at his rigid profile. "Don't tell me you're not running any more. You know that's not healthy."

He looked back at her. "I am running ragged around the hospital. Does that count?"

Gawd, I could get lost in his blue eyes. A flash of jealousy for those he worked with came upon her. *Do any of them flirt with him?*

Reaching the park, they found a grassy spot under the shade of some oak trees to spread their blanket—the same one they'd lain on to study in college this past spring. Jillian pulled out her magazines to peruse while David read his medical books. *Boring!*

He seemed better that morning when he woke up, certainly not irritable like he was yesterday afternoon. She knew from the plate in the sink that he had gotten up sometime during the night. She reasoned that if she was getting by on a few hours of sleep a day, she too would be bitchy.

"I'll be heading out on Tuesday morning. I'm flying to Arizona and then on to California. My last stop will be New York before I come home in two weeks," she said. "I've been gone so much this summer that when I finally stop travelling, I'll probably feel like I am invading Tara's space."

"Has she said anything to you?" David asked, not looking up from his book.

"No, but I am sure I'd feel that way if my roommate was gone so much and then suddenly was there all the time. It would drive me bananas."

"As tight as you and Tara are, I doubt you get on each other's nerves. But if you do, you could get a teaching job here."

"We've been through this before." She sighed and poked him in the shoulder. "You know I can't break my school contract."

"I know." He looked at her. He was lying on his side, the book in front of him still open to a picture of a heart. "It's just…"

"Just what?" she asked.

When he looked to the side and didn't answer right away, she got an uneasy feeling.

"It's just I like having you here. I don't want us to grow apart. That's all. You've been jet-setting all over this summer. Once school starts up, we'll probably see each other less. I wonder if I should be worried."

"Worried about what?"

"About us." He sat up. His face was all seriousness.

"I don't understand." She was not liking where this was going. Was he having doubts?

"Look at you Jillian. You're a beautiful woman surrounded by beautiful people. You're friendly and kind to everyone you meet. I am worried that while we're apart, someone will steal your heart."

Was he jealous?

She lifted her left hand. "Do you see this ring?" she asked. "It means, I love you and I want to marry you, you big dope."

His serious face relaxed a little.

She leaned over to kiss him. "When I'm traveling, I think of you and wish you were with me. I'm not interested in anyone else but you, so stop this crazy talk. I might sic Tara on you, and look what she did last time she thought you got me upset."

"You're right. I was over-thinking this," he said.

"Yes you were. Now do I have to ask if there is anything I should be worried about? I mean you are very easy on the eyes and you *are* a doctor."

"I'm not a doctor yet."

"You know what I mean."

"No, there's no one," he said gravely, before lying back down on the blanket. "Plus when would I have time to even notice someone?"

She wasn't sure if she should be concerned with his response or let it go. Quickly remembering what she'd had to go through to have him notice her, she realized he was largely oblivious to what happened around him. This knowledge relaxed her.

Chapter 14

The bell rang, signaling the end of the school day. Jillian's second graders were even aware it was going to be a long weekend and had barely been able to sit still after lunch. She could only imagine what it would be like in a few months for the long Thanksgiving weekend. At least her students behaved well walking down the hall toward the buses waiting to take them home.

She was going home to take a quick shower before she, Tara, and their neighbor Carol met for drinks at Tuxedo's. Since graduation they rarely hung out at their old college spots, though they'd found themselves at Gilly's last Friday. They wanted to be grown up, or at least try to be.

When she pulled into Tuxedo's parking lot, Carol had already snagged them an outside table with an umbrella. Carol worked as a freelance writer and had the most flexible hours of anyone Jillian knew. She was always the first to arrive anywhere. Whenever Jillian couldn't sleep and sat out on the balcony, she'd see the lights on in Carol's apartment.

Tara pulled into a parking spot a few spaces down. When she exited the car, she slammed the door with such force that Jillian was certain it came off its hinges.

"What's the matter?" Jillian knew Tara needed to vent something. She wouldn't cease until everything was off her chest, at which point she would announce she felt much better, and then life would go back to normal.

"I can't stand it anymore. I hate the people I work with. They are driving me crazy. Absolutely crazy. I don't think a single one of them has a personality," Tara exclaimed. They walked to the table where Carol was waiting.

"Hey, Carol." Jillian sat down.

Carol looked at the two of them. "Hello. Is everything okay?" Carol, originally from St. Louis, was several years older and sometimes acted as their mentor.

One night, over too many drinks, Jillian told the very petite, creamy-skinned, strawberry blonde that she looked like Tinkerbell. Instead of being offended, Carol laughed. The next time they went out she wore a tight green mini-skirt and green top.

Tara sat. "I officially hate my job. I'd give anything to be on a beach somewhere with a barely clad, and very built, man feeding me grapes."

Jillian signaled to the waiter. Drinks were desperately needed.

"It can't be that bad." Carol sat back in her chair.

"It is. I feel like a zombie sitting at my desk all day playing with debits and credits. Today, I mentioned I was going to happy hour and asked if anyone wanted to join. Well, you shoulda seen the looks I got. You woulda thought I asked them to give me all their money. All I heard the next hour was how expensive and fattening drinks are, not to mention the whining about hangovers. Ugh!" she exclaimed.

The waiter, poised with pen, asked, "May I take

your orders?"

"Well, hello there." Tara said looking up at the man. "I will have…"

Jillian held her breath wondering what she would say.

"A strawberry margarita."

Jillian sighed quietly. She had expected to hear the word "you." She barely looked at him. "I'll have the same with a glass of ice water. And can we get a bowl of chips and salsa?"

Tara was still batting her eyes. Flirt mode was in the high-alert zone. "And some cheese fries."

"Certainly."

After he walked away, Tara leaned back in her chair. "Don't say it Jilly. I shouldn't eat the fries, but my week sucked and I need some fattening food with my alcohol."

"Did I say anything?"

"No, but I know you were thinking it."

"Maybe. So back to you and your job. What are you going to do?"

Tara looked to where their waiter was. "Really, I would like to have him for a night. You know, to take my mind off my life right now."

Carol glanced his way, too. "I think he's younger than you."

"Both of you need to stop before I find another table to sit at. So, other than junior, what do you want?" Jillian asked.

"I don't know," Tara said. "Wait, I take that back. I want a body like yours, without having to exercise, and I would like a boyfriend."

"Careful, what you wish for," Carol said.

"Well, I would. I know this sounds so cliché, but I want someone who will treat me like a princess and think about me when I'm not around.

"You'll have your wish one day." Jillian smiled as the waiter put their drinks in front of them.

Tara took a sip of her frozen beverage. "Do you think David thinks about you when you're not there?"

Jillian didn't answer right away—not because she didn't know the answer, because it wasn't the one she wanted to accept.

"Jillian?" Tara looked directly at her.

"How come I have never met this elusive David?" Carol took a chip from the basket and dipped it in the salsa.

"He's in Knoxville, works crazy hours, and our schedules don't quite mesh."

Tara arched her right eyebrow at Jillian.

"I just asked since I've known you both for almost two months, and I've never seen him. And you know I know all that goes on in our building," Carol stated matter-of-factly before taking a sip of her beer.

Carol's apartment overlooked the front parking lot so she had a clear shot of anyone coming and going to their unit.

Carol looked Jillian in the eye. "Hey, didn't mean to get you upset. I just don't want to see you get hurt, like I was. You are beautiful—okay, beyond beautiful—and I'd hate to see anyone take advantage of you."

Jillian held her head high, "Oh, he's not taking advantage of me. It's just he's about three hours away, and our schedules are pretty mismatched."

"David's a good guy. He would never think of

hurting my friend here." Tara patted the table for emphasis. "But he does sometimes get so caught up in what's he doing he forgets about other things." She looked back to Jillian. "One thing I know for sure, he's in love with her. I can tell by the messages he leaves. Anyway, last time I thought he'd hurt Jilly here, the day ended with his eye blackened."

"Okay, I guess one bodyguard's enough, when she's this tough." Carol lifted her beer bottle to her lips. "I'd love to hear about this black eye."

"Some other time." Jillian just wanted the subject to end. David's absence was bugging her.

The last time she saw him was the beginning of July when she'd spent that weekend with him. Though they talked, the phone calls were few and far between. It felt as if she spoke more to his answering machine than him. It was hardest when a whole week had gone by and she didn't hear from him.

"Omigosh, is that Eric?" Jillian was glad for the distraction, but seeing him made her wish to see David. The two guys had been as inseparable as she and Tara.

Tara turned around in her chair. "It certainly is."

They waved at Eric, and he came over to the table to kiss the two roommates' cheeks. "If it isn't my two most favorite women in the world," he said.

Batting her eyelashes, Tara actually blushed.

"What are you doing here?" Jillian asked.

"Celebrating not working on a Friday night. That's a rarity." He pulled a chair from the nearby table and sat. "I live nearby, and I'm meeting up with some friends."

Carol leaned forward, extending her hand, "I'm Carol."

Tara jumped in. "Carol, this is Eric. He went to UK with us, and was David's roommate."

Eric shook her hand. "Pleasure to meet you."

"Funny, I was just asking Jillian and Tara if this David-guy really existed. I've never seen the man," Carol said candidly.

Jillian winced a little from Carol's brusqueness.

Carol was still trying to mend a broken heart and thought all relationships were doomed. Finally relenting to her boyfriend's wishes, she had followed him from St. Louis only to have him dump her after four months.

"Oh he exists. I saw him a week ago. Several of us went to Nashville and hung out for a few days. Okay, some if it was more like a drunk-fest, but it was fun."

Tara asked, "Really?"

"The only downer was someone had stupidly said something to Cathy, so of course she was there. She kept chastising us for our immaturity. The best part of the trip was when David told her to shut-up."

What? David and Cathy were in Nashville? How come this was the first time Jillian was hearing of this?

Eric stared at her before continuing. "Didn't he tell you he was going? We asked him how you were and if you were joining us, but he said you were busy with school."

"No, I didn't know he was going." Jillian's stomach was in knots.

"Did Cathy behave herself?" Tara asked, looking intently at Eric.

"Yes. And to put your mind at ease, David roomed with me, and he was in bed alone every night so you have no reason to worry there. Cathy, of course, tried to convince him that being engaged, and eventually married, would impinge on his future freedom of meeting up with us."

Carol shook her beer bottle to see how much was left. "Hate to butt into this, but Jillian, are you sure marrying him is the right thing? The look on your face shows you're having some misgivings. You need to make sure you're really ready for this."

"Let's not talk about this anymore, okay?" Jillian said. "He probably told me, and I just forgot about it as I focused on lesson plans."

"That's probably it," Tara said.

Eric reached out to squeeze her shoulder. "He loves you, you know."

"I know."

The waiter appeared to ask if they wanted refills. Eric ordered a beer and ended up staying with them the rest of the night.

****

Later that night, when Jillian and Tara pulled into the parking lot, Carol bolted from the back seat of Jillian's car.

"I think I'm going to be sick," Carol said, before proceeding to empty the contents of her stomach on the hood of the car parked alongside.

"Oh, Jeez, we better clean that up before the owner of the car sees it," Tara said, holding her nose.

Carol groaned. "Why did you let me do all those shots with your friend?"

Jillian looked into the back seat where Eric was slumped against the door.

"Do you think we should leave him there?" Jillian wondered how she and Tara were going to get him up to their apartment.

"I'm tempted," Tara said, watching Carol. "Leave him for now, anyway. We need to clean up that car."

Carol stood up straight and started to stumble toward the building's stairwell.

"Let's help her first and then get some buckets of water. Eric drew the last straw," Jillian said.

Tara and Jillian got on either side of the unsteady, weaving Carol to guide her up the stairs.

Once Carol was snug in her bed, with a trashcan set nearby, they went to their apartment and filled one bucket with soapy water and another of clear for rinsing. On the way back to the parking lot, they started to laugh when the water sloshed over the bucket rims. The harder they tried to be quiet, the louder they became.

Jillian dumped the soapy water on the hood. Just as Tara was about to pour the clean water, they heard a very agitated and distinctly male voice ask, "What are you doing to my new car?"

"Our neighbor threw up on it, so we're cleaning it for you." Tara upended the bucket to allow all the water to run down.

Jillian looked at the car and then back to the tall man. He was almost the same height as Jillian with wavy, bordering on curly, blond hair. His studious glasses reminded her of the New York City marketing executive who always asked her to dinner when she was in town.

Mr. Agitation glowered at his car. "Are you flippin' out of your minds?"

Before Jillian could speak, Tara's hand was on her hip. "Listen Buck-O, we were doing a good deed, here. Which would you prefer? An inadequately washed car?

Or one with vomit on the hood?"

"I would've preferred that whoever it was had puked somewhere else."

"Is that so? Honestly, I liked it that she waited and did it outside our car, because if she'd done it inside, my friend over here"—Tara pointed her thumb in Jillian's direction—"would have had a fit. And I have to live with her. So there."

The man said nothing but looked back and forth at the two of them. "I guess you're right," he finally relented.

"Damn right we are," Tara said saucily.

"I think you missed a spot." He pointed. "Let me help, so it's done right."

"Control freak," Tara whispered under her breath.

Jillian looked to the pair. She had to go pee but wondered if it was safe to leave Tara alone with this man they'd just met.

As if reading her mind, he said, "I am Peter. Peter Reid. I live on the third floor."

"Tara Spencer. And this is my friend and roommate, Jillian O'Malley."

He gave each a firm handshake. "Nice meeting you," he said.

Jillian looked back at her own car to see Eric sleeping with his mouth open. She needed to take care of him.

"If you two are okay taking care of the car without me, I'm going to get Eric up to the apartment."

Tara spun around, "Omigawd, I totally forgot about him."

Peter looked in the car, too. "Give me a few minutes here, and I can help you."

"Thanks," Tara answered sweetly, laying on the charm. She helped Peter clean up his car, while Jillian ran to the apartment and back after relieving herself.

They roused Eric enough to get him out of the car. A few unrecognizable words slurred from his lips as Tara and Peter guided him up the three flights of stairs to their apartment.

Opening the door, Jillian ran to her room to get an extra pillow and blanket for Eric, whom had been deposited on their couch.

"I should probably get him a glass of water." Jillian looked down at him snoring.

"Let him be, but keep the bathroom light on in case he needs it," Peter said.

"Thanks for the help," Jillian said,

"Yes, thank you. And sorry about your car," Tara added.

"My pleasure…the helping, not the car. See you around," Peter said before leaving.

When the door shut, Tara looked at Jillian, "He's cute. I think I can like him."

"How about we talk about this in the morning?" Jillian said. "I'm going to bed."

"I like polka dot panties," Eric slurred in his sleep.

Jillian and Tara exchanged surprised looks and started to laugh.

****

When Jillian walked back into the apartment after dropping a very hungover Eric at his place and Carol at her car, Tara was sitting on the patio with her knees pressed up to her body. She looked up with a serious face.

"Is everything okay?" Jillian asked.

"Other than I barely got any sleep? Even though I used to sleep with him, I never remember Eric snoring like that before."

"He probably didn't do five shots of tequila with I don't know how many beer chasers when you were dating."

"That's true. But I was sitting here thinking, we really never dated. We had a good time together, but it wasn't dating. In fact if you think of it, I hardly date."

"You are a serial dater." Jillian sat in the glider they'd taken from Nana's garage. "What's going on Tara? You're not yourself."

"I was thinking back to our conversation yesterday at Tuxedo's and then about meeting Peter last night, or earlier this morning if you want to get technical." Tara picked up her coffee mug to take a drink.

"Okay." Jillian was unsure of where this conversation was going.

"You're right. I'm a serial dater who is in it only for the sex. While I want sex with Peter, I also want to get to know him. If you think about it, he was really gentlemanly last night, helping us with Eric after he calmed down about his car."

Tara sat up straight and looked at Jillian. "Not once did I feel like he was staring at my boobs. Do you think he's gay?"

"No, I don't think he is. So what's the problem?"

"He's a nice guy. I don't want to come on too strong and blow it. I'd like something like you and David have."

"I'm not sure you should aspire to that. I mean look at us. It's been almost two months since we've seen each other."

"I'm sorry Jillian. I know this is tearing you up inside. I wish I could help, but you know what I mean by having that type of love."

"Well to start, keep your panties on until after the tenth date. Get the guy to know the Tara that we all love."

"What? Ten dates? Do you want me to enter a convent, too?"

"No, I'm just saying get to know the person before you get to know them physically."

"Omigawd, you are no fun."

"What do you want me to say? 'Bang him'?"

Tara started to laugh and hit her leg, "Good one!"

"So I don't have the lingo down."

"Well you shouldn't. You are a respectable second grade teacher who has to instill morals in our future generation. We can't have them going home saying anything inappropriate."

Tara took another sip of her coffee. "Fine. I'll try it, but if I get cranky, you'll know why. And then I'll resort to eating a whole carton of ice cream *with* a bag of cookies, and you know that, unlike yours, my thighs and butt will expand."

"No they won't. You are exaggerating?"

"Am I? We have known each other five years now, and your size and weight haven't changed, while I've dressed in every possible size from a two to a ten. I've been on more diets than you and I together can count. If I add up all the weight I've lost in the five years, I shouldn't even exist right now. It is so not fair."

"What's not fair? I watch every morsel I eat and work out to keep it off. This isn't easy for me. There is nothing I would love more than to eat and not worry about the scale," Jillian said in a huff. She was sick to death of the comments about her weight.

"I'm sorry, Jillian." Tara stood. "I'm just having a pity party."

"It's okay. Let's just make sure there are no sweets in here."

"Just great! No sex *and* no sugar! What is a poor girl to do?" Tara rolled her eyes. "Do you want any coffee, since I'm up?"

"Is there enough?"

"I think so," Tara said loudly from the kitchen.

When the doorbell rang, Tara looked out at Jillian. "Expecting anyone? Carol usually yells over from her balcony to say she's on her way."

"She's hung over, too, and can't take loud noise." Jillian walked inside.

When Tara opened the door, Peter was there.

"Hey, just wanted to stop by to see if everyone was okay."

Tara's smile broadened. "That is so nice of you. Yes, we are up. But naps will be needed this afternoon since Eric's snoring was like a rusty lawnmower."

"Is he still here?"

"No, Jillian dropped him off a little while ago."

"Hey Jillian." Peter gave her a half-hearted wave.

"Hey Peter."

Peter's voice took on a reserved tone. "So Tara, I was wondering if you had plans this evening."

Jillian stepped back out onto the patio and closed the door to give them privacy. Out of the corner of her eye, she saw Tara invite him inside. The two stood near the breakfast bar talking.

Tara kept nervously running her hands through her

hair, quite out of character. She wrote something on the pad of paper and handed it to him. There seemed to be lots of smiles before he exited the front door.

Jillian opened the patio slider.

"Well?"

"We're going to play miniature golf and then head over to the Cat's Hat where his cousin's band is performing tonight." With a squeal, Tara said, "I think he likes me."

Gone was the earlier disheartened Tara.

"Okay, this counts as date number one. Just nine more to go after tonight."

Tara threw the kitchen towel at her. "Who's counting?"

"Me," Jillian said. "Now let's pick you out something to wear."

Chapter 15

Rubbing the back of his tense neck, David walked into the doctors' lounge in the maternity ward. He knew from this rotation that the one field he would never specialize in was obstetrics. He gave credit to all the doctors and nurses who found satisfaction in this. He was sure not one of them. It made him reflect on his desire to have children when he and Jillian married.

Thinking of Jillian, he needed to call her and have her come down for a weekend. Eric had informed him that he had told Jillian of their recent trip to Nashville. Though she hadn't appeared to be phased, Eric had noticed an exchanged look between her and Tara.

David came to a stop at the magazine-littered table by the couches. The top one had Jillian on the cover. He was overcome by the sight of her green eyes, high cheek bones, and Mona Lisa smile. Her black hair was a mess, but he knew from the one time he was with her on a shoot, that they probably spent an hour to get her hair to look like that. And, of course, they had fans blowing on her.

He picked up the magazine and thumbed through the pages to see where she was featured.

Bill and Sally, two other residents on the same rotation as he, came into the lounge. Sally fell backward on the couch, "I'm beyond tired. I don't know why a woman would want to get pregnant and go through this. When I decide to settle down, I'm adopting…a dog."

David briefly glanced at her to nod, before continuing his pursuit of finding more Jillian photos.

Bill stood next to him, "Seriously man, what are you doing? Please don't give me the line about reading that trash to understand the female psyche."

David ignored him as he found the spread of Jillian showcasing upcoming fall fashions.

Bill looked over his shoulders. "I tried to read this garbage once, but it made me laugh. It's women writing articles on how to make a man fall in love with them, or how to satisfy your man so he doesn't wander. But my all-time favorite is how to *think* like a man. Seems like they'd need a man writing that, not a woman."

Sally turned her head to look at them. "You are such a sexist, Bill."

David held up the magazine in front of him. "This is my fiancée on the cover."

Bill leaned back with a dubious expression. "Dude, you are suffering from sleep deprivation if you're saying things like that. You can dream about them, but you can't go around talking like that. Someone will think you've gone nuts."

Bill grabbed the magazine from his hands, "She is hot. Good choice for a fantasy. I think I'll make her my girlfriend in tonight's dreams. You don't mind sharing, do you?"

"Yes, I do. I mean it. Jillian and I are engaged." David snatched the magazine back from Bill to flip to the pages in the middle.

"See this ring?" He pointed to two of the pictures. "I gave it to her at her graduation party."

Sally stood up from the couch. "Let me see this. Wow, she's beautiful. So how, exactly, did you two meet?"

"At UK. She and her roommate literally ran into me."

Bill asked, "So where is she and how come you've never brought her around?"

"She's a school teacher in Lexington. She'll be looking for a position here next year."

"Wait. She's a school teacher. And a model? Davey, you're getting a little carried away with this delusion of yours."

"Her modeling contract expired the end of August, and she didn't renew it. Once it was done, she started her teaching job," he replied matter-of-factly.

Sally studied him. "Bill, I don't think he's deranged or even kidding us. That's a big change from model to teacher."

"I'm telling you this"—Bill looked at the pictures again—"if I was engaged to her, I wouldn't let her out of my sight. Ever. I wouldn't want men ogling her."

Sally said, "Like you are right now?" She looked back at David. "I have to say, I never thought you had a girlfriend with all the hours you work."

"I thought you were seeing that girl, what's-her-name. The one who's been up here a few times with the big glasses and tight ponytail." Bill handed the magazine over to Sally.

"Cathy is just a friend. She was in medical school with me at UK."

"Does she know about your fiancée?" Bill asked.

"More importantly, does your fiancée know about her?" Sally asked.

"Yes to both."

"So help me understand. How is it we've never met your fiancée, but we have met your female friend from medical school?" Bill asked.

"Jillian's been busy, and with our schedules, it's been difficult. She has weekends off, and I don't."

"You should still have her come out, so we can meet her…just to be sure this is real," Bill said.

Sally shook her head, "No, *you* want her here to find out if she has a sister."

Bill sat on the couch. "A model! David, you are the man. I need to do whatever it is you are doing to get a girl like that."

David looked again at the cover of the magazine. He was going to buy a copy after work. "I'll give her a call, and you can meet her." Seeing her made him realize how long it had been, and how much he missed having her near. Talking on the phone wasn't enough. He would call as soon as his shift was over. He didn't need these two listening to his conversation.

Chapter 16

It took David and Jillian longer than expected to leave the hospital. His plan had been simple—introduce Jillian to his colleagues and then head back to his apartment. However, it seemed there were quite a number of folks who wanted to meet his mysterious fiancée.

There were only two uncomfortable times when someone commented that they had no idea he was engaged. When it happened the second time, Jillian cocked her head to the side and gave him a questioning look. He shrugged it off, but he could literally see the wheels in her head turning.

When they reached her car in the parking lot, he pressed her up against the passenger door to kiss her deeply. Running his arms along her lean body, his own reacted. They needed to leave quickly before any of his nosy colleagues saw him in this unprofessional state of arousal.

Once inside the apartment, Jillian said, "Thank you for the roses. They are beautiful."

"Not as beautiful as you." He dropped the keys on the counter, grabbed her wrist, and pulled her up against him.

At times like this, he liked that she was almost as tall as him. He never had to bend over to kiss her. Her hands were immediately running over his face and through his hair. David pulled back to look into her green eyes.

"It was so wrong to have gone this long," he whispered. Nibbling on her ear lobe and then kissing the spot below ear, he made a trail down her neck.

"I was wondering when you were going to come to your senses," she whispered back, pushing her chest into his.

He lifted her slim body, carried her into the bedroom, and placed her gently on the bed. When she tried to sit up, he shook his hands. He quickly took off his shirt and lay with her.

Sliding his hands under her silk blouse, he felt her lace bra. Rubbing his fingers over her nipples, he felt them harden, just like himself.

Her fingers undid his pants to free the building pressure. "I see someone is ready." She radiated a lazy smile before pushing his pants down.

"I don't want to rush." David rolled to the side to kick his pants off, now clad only in his boxers. Jillian was still fully clothed.

"You look awfully sexy like this," she said.

Slowly he unbuttoned her top, observing her quickened breathing. He kissed each spot he revealed. When he saw her black lacy bra, he knew it was a good thing he hadn't been aware of this at the hospital. He would have had to misappropriate one of the rooms.

He unsnapped her jeans to see her matching lace panties. He lost all control, yanking her jeans off and tossing them on the floor. His mouth started at her breasts and continued downward. He wanted to taste all of her and hear her moan his name. When he was done, he hovered over her body, kissing her neck and her lips.

Jillian circled her legs around him, pulling herself to him. "Please David," she pleaded. "I want you now."

"And I always want you," he managed to articulate as he thrust into her.

Her thighs clenched around him, and she ran her nails along his back. Burying her face in his neck, she screamed his name, and they climaxed together. When the last shiver of her orgasm finished, he lay on top of her, sweaty and satisfied. After a while, he rolled off and held her in his arms.

Jillian immediately flipped her leg onto one of his and ran her fingers over his chest. "I'm sorry that you had to do all the work there," she said apologetically.

"What are you talking about," he asked, stroking her shoulder.

"I got all the pleasure, and I did nothing for you."

The sparkling gleam in her eyes was hypnotizing. "Jillian, I love making love to you. I love tasting every part of you, and being inside of you. You are incredible, and I couldn't ask for more, so stop saying that."

She rested her chin on his chest, "Okay. So, tell me this. Did you want to show me off or something at the hospital?"

"I did."

"Why?"

"When I saw you on the cover of *Glamour* and told them you were my fiancée, they didn't believe me." He continued to stroke her back with his fingers. "Anyway, it had been way too long since we had seen each other, and I missed you."

"I was actually starting to wonder if you'd forgotten about me."

"Never. You know you don't need to wait to be

invited. You have a key. Come whenever. I want you here and can't wait until it's permanent."

"Speaking of that…don't you think we should set a date?"

His fingers stopped their movements on her back.

"What?" she asked.

"I don't want to be poverty-stricken when we marry, Jillian. I don't want to be the clichéd newlyweds living in a one-bedroom apartment."

"We won't be, David. I have money saved, and I work, too."

"I don't want to have my wife support me. I want to financially stand on my own two feet."

"Aren't you now?"

"I'm barely making ends meet as I pay off my student loans."

"Once we get married, my money is your money. No one needs to know how much each of us contributes to the household."

"I'll know."

"So are you saying we aren't getting married next year?"

"I'd like to wait two years, Jillian."

Her eyes were hard when she sat up. "Are you kidding me?"

"I just want to be a little more financially secure."

"You know I can't live with you before we get married. My family, well my Nana especially, would have a fit if I was to live with a guy. They didn't raise me like that. And I don't want that either."

Sitting up, he took her hands in his and brought them to his lips. He scooted her naked body close to his, wanting her to wrap her legs around him.

"I won't ask you to do anything you don't want. Just give me two years. That's all I'm asking. I'll have saved up by then, and we can buy a house."

Her sad eyes only stared at him.

"I love you, Jillian. I want to spend the rest of my life with you. But I also want to be the one to provide for you. I'd be miserable otherwise, and that wouldn't be fair to you."

He leaned forward to kiss her pouty lips. At first they were unyielding, but the more he kissed and teased with his tongue, the more she responded. He ran his hands over her perky breasts and felt himself get hard again. By the time he ran his fingers lower, she was ready and relaxed, her body no longer anxious and tense. When they made love the second time, it was intense and passionate.

She cuddled into him afterward. "We'll get married in eighteen months. All you need to do is show up. Tara, Nana, and I will handle all the details.

"Okay."

****

There was nothing better than being snuggled up against David. Jillian watched him sleep. There were times she wished he'd smile more; he was so serious. In sleep, he looked at peace. Though she should let him sleep as they'd been up most of the night talking, making love, dozing off, and repeating the cycle, she wanted to touch him. Gently, she brushed her hands over his face and then across his wide shoulders. Her fingers continued along his arm before retracing her path.

Without opening his eyes, he asked, "What are you doing?"

"Nothing." She pushed her body closer to his. Her fingers trailed over him noticing how hard and ready he was. She continued to stroke him.

Just as his hands reached to pull her closer, his phone rang from the other room. They lay still.

A female voice came on the machine. "David. It's your mom…"

David jumped from the bed to grab the phone.

Jillian snatched the shirt he had worn to work yesterday off the floor. Pulling it around her, she followed him to the living room.

He ran his free hand through his hair and left it at the base of his neck. Any serenity witnessed earlier was gone. "We'll be there as soon as we can," he said, looking back to her.

She took that as her cue to jump in the shower to get ready to leave. As she was rinsing the soap from her body, David walked into the bathroom.

"That was my mom. My father's not doing well. She's asked me to come check on him since he's too stubborn to pay to see a doctor." He paused, "I, um, wondered if you would come with me."

"Of course." She stepped from the shower, trading places with him.

Jillian walked into the kitchen, wrapped in her towel, to start a pot of coffee. They were going to need it after not getting much sleep. On a good day neither one was functional until they'd had at least two cups. With to-go cups, they left in David's Jeep to head to eastern Kentucky.

He was silent for most of the trip. Several times, Jillian offered to drive so he could sleep. Each time he declined with one-word responses. She passed the time looking out the window.

When they pulled off the highway, he finally spoke a complete sentence. "My mom thinks this is the end. She wants me to make peace with him before he dies."

"That's the right thing to do," Jillian replied.

David shook his head, never taking his eyes from the road. "She called 9-1-1, but my father wouldn't let them inside."

At a stop light, he turned to her, "I'm going just to say goodbye. Nothing else. I'm doing this for my mom, not for him."

"I understand," she said.

"I don't think you will, until you meet him. He's nothing like your father."

Jillian had no response to that, and he said nothing further. The silence in the car was unnerving. She knew idle chatter would not put him at ease.

She wondered what it must be like to visit a dying man, your father, out of obligation instead of caring and love. She looked at David's handsome, but ever-rigid face. Now it looked so tense, it might shatter into a million pieces. How was she going to pick them all up?

"I need to warn you about something. My parents still live in the same trailer where I grew up. Back then, it was pretty run-down and dilapidated. I'm certain it's gotten worse."

"Okay."

"It's poverty at its worst. After you see it, I don't want your pity. And don't show any to my parents, either. My father will sense it, and he can say cruel things. Thankfully, if my mom's right, he won't be around much longer to have to deal with."

She reached over, took his hand, and brought it to

her lips.

David took a sharp right onto a trailer-lined dirt road. Some of the mobile homes looked abandoned, and the ones showing signs of habitants were pretty ramshackle. They stopped at the end of the dirt road, and Jillian stared at the old, barely-standing trailer. On the roof, rocks held down a large sheet of plastic, the indentation of the hole it was covering was visible. Some of the windows were duct-taped to keep them from falling out.

Where a yard might have been was overrun with brush. In the corner an old vehicle had a large weed growing out the open driver's window. Though David had warned her, Jillian was sure they'd made a wrong turn. She glanced at him. His hard face was void of emotion.

She touched his arm and smiled at him. Before departing the safety of the car, she mouthed, "I love you."

Taking her hand, he approached the door, which didn't seem to be able to close properly. One of the hinges was probably loose and needed tightening. If Jillian hadn't been told otherwise, she would have assumed this place to be abandoned. Surely no one actually lived here. The smell of garbage and decay permeated the surrounding vegetation.

The door opened before David knocked. The woman standing before them looked prematurely old, the result of poverty and neglect. Her wrinkled face was framed by stringy gray hair, her thin lips pressed into a permanent frown. Her vacant blue eyes held only grief. A semblance of a smile crossed her face as she looked at her son standing before her.

"David?" she croaked.

"Mom. This is Jillian. I told you about her."

When the withered woman looked at her, Jillian wondered if his mother had ever been happy. No one ever expects their life to come to this. She felt a heaviness in her stomach, but she looked the woman in the eye, and smiled. "Hello, Mrs. Rainier. Nice to meet you."

A deep voice came from inside the trailer. "Leigh, who's at the door? Ya better not have called nine-one-one again. I warned ya what I'd do if ya did. Yer gonna regret it this time."

There was a look of fear and embarrassment in Leigh's face. David, never releasing Jillian's hand, walked into the trailer. In fact, his hand tightened around hers.

David's voice was hard. "It's me." He looked at his father lying on the couch. "I see you haven't moved since the last time I saw you."

Jillian almost screamed when a large mouse scurried by. Instead she moved closer to David.

"Well, well, well, if it ain't my son, the doctor. Ya have to excuse me; I didn't hear your Mercedes pull up. Ya killed anyone lately?" He sneered before a deadly-sounding cough wracked his body.

In a soft, but controlled, voice David responded, "How are you?"

Before he could reply the coughing started again.

Leigh hurried over with a washrag and held it to his face.

Jillian stood quietly, without moving or blinking. She watched the old man's body heave with each cough—a painful sound that cut through the unnatural silence in the trailer.

David asked, "Why haven't you gone to a doctor?"

"You're the one who did this to me. After you killed Todd, I hadda drink to forget what ya did."

"I made you drink?" David asked angrily. "I'm not the one who held the bottle to your lips. I seem to remember you drinking long before he died."

Jillian looked at the man she loved. It startled her to hear him talk in this cold way.

At that moment the father became aware of her. His cold eyes sent a chill up her spine. "Who's this?" he demanded.

"My fiancée, Jillian."

The old man managed an evil laugh, immediately followed with more of the hideous coughing.

"Is that a fact now?" He glanced at Jillian. "You pregnant? Or just plain stupid to want to marry him?" His body was once again wracked with coughs.

The tone of David's response surprised her. "I'm used to your insults, but leave her out of this. This is between you and me. No one else."

Jillian felt David's grip tighten on her hand. She thought he was going to crush her fingers.

The old man looked back at her. "Ya know he's got nothin' to offer you. Or are ya waiting around until he's a big ol' fancy doctor?" He nodded his head as though pleased with himself. "Maybe, yer not so stupid after all. Ya better watch yerself, though." He leaned forward as though to tell her a secret. "He's a way of killin' people and then actin' all innocent."

David let go of her hand and stood right over his father. "Shut up, you son of a bitch! You know exactly what happened to Todd."

Jillian looked at the father and then at David. Years of disgruntlement and disgust exuded from their eyes as they glared at each other. Neither was going to back down.

Leigh started to cry. Through her tears, she looked despairingly at the two men. "Why can't you make peace with each other?"

"I intended to, but not if he insults Jillian," David said vehemently.

Jillian had never seen David like this. She looked at him and mouthed the words, "It's okay." Her mouth felt dry. She needed to get out of this confined space. She walked over to Leigh. "Let's go outside," she whispered.

Like a lost puppy, Leigh followed her to the two old chairs in the front yard. Jillian first tested the chair for sturdiness before sitting and then wiped the dirt and leaves from it.

She bit her lip before turning to Leigh. "How long has he been like this?"

Leigh pulled out a pack of cigarettes and lit up. She put the cigarette to her lips and inhaled deeply. She exhaled the smoke above her head. "Being mean, or the coughing?"

"Both."

"Jake's been mean ever since Todd, our youngest, was born. Todd meant another mouth to feed. His coughing has worsened over the past few months. We've got no money for him to see a doctor, plus he refuses to go. He wants to make sure there's enough money for his whiskey. He drinks and then passes out. He's only awake a couple of hours a day. I usually sit out here so I don't have to be around him. I figure it's his life, so it doesn't..." She looked away and took several deep drags of her cigarette.

"I guess I don't understand why you didn't leave him."

"Leave him? Are you kidding me? You and I wouldn't be sitting here talking today if I left him. David and I would be rotting in the earth. When the boys were younger, I was scared for their safety. I left him once. I ran to my momma's house." She stopped to throw her cigarette on the ground. "Jake found us and shot up her house. Hit Momma in the leg. Told me if I ever left again, he'd shoot David and make me watch him die."

She pulled out another smoke and again inhaled deeply before continuing. "David was my favorite. Growing up, he was a good boy. He was so smart and never gave me an ounce of trouble. Not like his brother, Todd. Todd was just like Jake, mean to the bone. Even looked like him. Todd could do no wrong in his father's eyes. I was always being called to the school because of trouble with him."

Tears formed in Leigh's eyes, and her bottom lip quivered. "I'll never forget the time that I praised David for being so good and considerate." She wiped her nose with the back of her hand.

"What happened?" Jillian was scared of what she was going to hear.

"That night when the boys were asleep, Jake dragged David from his bed, took him outside, and beat him within an inch of his life. I ran and got in between. He beat me, too. I remember looking up and seeing Todd standing in the doorway, doing nothing."

Jillian's stomach lurched, and she covered her

mouth with her hand. She looked back to the trailer, before turning her attention again to this sad woman. The pain, evident in her eyes, stabbed at Jillian's heart. "It will be over soon."

"I'm so accustomed to this life I don't know what I will do when he leaves. Isn't that horrible? You would think I'd be happy to finally be free of him. What will I do?" It was more a statement than a question.

Leigh threw her cigarette to the ground and stubbed it out with her foot. "When are you getting married?"

"In a year-and-a-half.

"Help my son heal. Help him make peace with his past."

They heard a loud bang, and they both turned as the door slammed closed. David's long, lean legs strode toward them in anger. He stopped in front of his mother, squatted, and took her hands in his.

His eyes filled with compassion as he spoke. "I'm sorry for you, Mom. Sorry you stay with him. He may rot in hell, for all I care. Pack your bags and leave with us today."

She looked over at Jillian who smiled and nodded her head in agreement. She gazed lovingly back at her son and put her hand to his face. Tearfully, she said, "I can't. You know that."

David looked away briefly before responding, "He won't last much longer. It's going to be a painful death."

Jillian stood when he did. Leigh rose from her chair and hugged her son. Jillian stood back, feeling sorry for her.

Leigh hugged her and whispered, "I wish the best

for you."

Jillian sat in the car and leaned her head against the back of the seat. She was spent after witnessing just a few minutes of this family's interactions. She looked at David's hard profile. She couldn't fathom the idea of being beaten by his father because he did not get into trouble at school.

As if reading her thoughts, David turned to look at her, "Let it go, Jillian. It's in the past."

"What did you and your father talk about in there?"

"I asked about his coughing. I wanted to know how long it had been going on. I acted like a doctor and he like a patient. I told him he would probably be dead in less than a week. He said that was fine, and that he would meet me in hell. Then I left."

Jillian stared out the window. Wasn't there a point you would ask for forgiveness to move forward with your life?

****

After stopping for sandwiches at the new deli that had opened around the corner, David was drained when they stepped back into the apartment. The last twenty hours had been more than taxing, starting with the screamer woman in labor, followed by the long drive to and from his parents. And don't forget to throw in the stress of interacting with his father. All he wanted was a quiet evening with Jillian before he returned to the hospital by six in the morning.

The answering machine light was blinking, and he figured it was his mother. He hit the play button before turning to join Jillian in the kitchen as she unloaded their food.

"Hey David. It's Cathy. I'm thinking of coming up

on Wednesday to spend—"

Like a flash, he was by the machine pressing the delete button.

The damage was done. Jillian's normally serene face was infuriated. "Why is Cathy calling you?" she asked tersely.

"It's nothing," he said.

This day was going from bad to worse.

The anger came clearly through her voice. "Nothing? I don't think her coming up to see you is 'nothing.' Does she know about us?"

"Yes."

"Then explain to me why she is coming up. And where does she stay?"

"Jillian, calm down. She and her roommates don't get along—"

"There's a surprise." Jillian crossed her arms across her chest.

"When she has two days off in a row, she likes to go somewhere."

"And is that 'somewhere' here?"

"She's only been up here twice."

The daggers coming from Jillian's eyes were enough to kill him. "Only twice? In case you have forgotten, we're engaged. I think that gives me every right to say this. She's not to stay here. I don't trust her. Not one bit. She wants you David, and I think you are blind to that. You have to make a choice. Her or me."

"Jillian. She's just a friend."

"Who *wants* you very badly. She's trying very hard to drive a wedge between you and me. I'm not saying it again."

"I choose you."

"Good answer," she said curtly.

It was going to take a lot to overcome the mood in the apartment. Jillian was still seething while they ate their dinner in silence. David sat next to her on the couch and tried to cradle her in his arms. This was met with a fair amount of resistance.

"I mean it David. Look what she did to us when we were at UK."

He kissed her forehead. "I remember. Like I said, I'll always choose you."

Chapter 17

It had been two weeks since Jillian's last visit, which had gone much better than the time before. She and David had spent the weekend driving around looking at houses that they might be able to afford one day, the different suburbs, and the schools where she might be able to teach.

Though it was never brought up, she knew his answering machine was off and his phone never rang.

David's father had since passed, and he had made the trip alone to be with this mother. He had asked his mom to move from the trailer, but she wouldn't.

Jillian was actually glad he'd asked her not to come. She felt sorry for his mother but was unable to relate to her in any meaningful way. She had been so sad that day they met.

Though Jillian knew he had to work, at the last minute she decided to drive down to Knoxville. The weather in Lexington was ideal and the crowds had descended upon Keeneland to watch the fall horse racing. It was a perfect time to make an exit.

It was dusk when she pulled into the apartment parking lot. David's car was there. She didn't remember him saying he was off. Had she known that she would have left home earlier.

She pulled her weekend bag from the car and walked up to his apartment. Using her key, she unlocked the door as quietly as she could, in case he was asleep. She whispered, "Hello? David?"

He came out of his room, freshly showered and dressed in a suit. She could smell his cologne—the one that drove her crazy.

He stopped in the doorway, surprised to see her. "Jillian!"

She whistled at him. "You're mighty dressed up."

He did not move from the doorway.

"Big plans for the night?" she asked suspiciously.

He looked at the floor in front of her feet, before answering. "Um. Yeah."

Something wasn't right. His voice was flat. Panicked, she asked, "What's wrong?"

"Just shocked to see you, that's all. I didn't know you were coming."

"I wanted to surprise you." She took a step toward him. He didn't move. "Don't jump up and down for joy. I might think you're excited to see me."

"Sorry. You just caught me off guard."

"David, can you help me with this?" Cathy walked from his bedroom.

Without her glasses and her hair down, Jillian almost didn't recognize her. She was stunning in a little black cocktail dress that plunged low to show her ample cleavage.

All the blood drained from Jillian's face. Her weekend bag felt heavy. She sucked in her lips to keep them from quivering. She tried to control the bile rising in her throat.

Looking from Cathy back to David, she hissed, "What is going on here?"

"Oh, hi Jillian. David invited me up for a cocktail

party being hosted—"

"Cathy, let me handle this." David's face gave away his guilt. He had been caught.

Jillian glared at both of them. "What is going on?"

She held her hand up to David's approach. "Stop. I asked you what's going on."

"When we talked, you said that a bunch of you were going to Keeneland this weekend. This came up, and I didn't want to take you away from that."

"David, you know I'd gladly drop Keeneland to be here with you. Look. I'm here now."

"Oh Jillian, you are so sweet, but sometimes naïve. You would've been bored with all this doctor-talk," Cathy said smugly. "Plus, it would be over your head."

"Shut-up Cathy. In fact, leave!" Jillian pointed to the door.

Cathy's mouthed formed an 'O.' Her eyes brightened. "Oh Jillian, what a beautiful ring on your finger. Who's the lucky guy?"

Jillian's brain froze.

"I am," David said harshly. "Now, can you give us some privacy?"

Cathy crossed her arms, "You didn't tell me that."

When David didn't answer her, she turned around, "Fine I'll go finish getting ready."

Jillian watched her walk back into the very room that she had no place being in. Her nose tingled with held-back tears. She had to hold herself together for what was turning into her worst nightmare.

"You better not lie to me. Have you slept with her?"

"No. Never," he responded quickly. Once again, David tried to close the distance between them.

Jillian took a step back. All she could do was glare at him. She felt sick. Her hands were sweaty. Her voice became icy cold, "Isn't it ironic that when a couple gets engaged, it's only the woman who wears a ring? The world knows she's taken, and is off limits. No one cares about the guy. He doesn't have the ball and chain tied to him yet. He can come and go as he pleases. It's especially easy for him when his fiancée lives in another state."

"It's not what you think, Jillian. Her boyfriend broke up with her this week. She called to tell me, and while we were talking, I told her about this cocktail party and who would be there. I thought it might cheer her up."

Jillian snapped back. "Isn't that convenient? Was there ever really a boyfriend? Or does she still have delusions that you two are meant to be together?"

She could feel her voice shaking. "David, you need to tell her to go."

From the bedroom, Cathy yelled sweetly, "David, we need to hurry up or we're going to be late. You said you wanted to be there at seven."

Jillian couldn't believe this. She thought she was going to hyperventilate. She somehow managed to speak. "You know I would have gone with you and socialized. I would have enjoyed the time because I was spending it with you, David." She paused and twisted the ring from her finger. She felt her nose starting to run from holding back the tears.

"Jillian, stop."

She shook her head. Her voice sounded flat to her own ears when she continued, "No. Don't come near me. At least let me walk out of here with some dignity."

She set the ring on the table near the door. "You're free, David. I hoped we'd have a happy life together, but I guess that was me being—what was it?—naïve."

She placed her hand on the doorknob and practically ran down the stairs.

He caught up with her as she was starting up her car. "Jillian, I love you," he said, hitting her window.

Jillian shook her head, in disgust, and put her car in drive. "I don't want to see or hear from you ever again. Do you hear me? Don't follow me. If you call me, I won't answer."

As she pulled from the parking lot, she looked in her rearview mirror to see him standing there. His shoulders drooped. His hands were on the top of his head.

Down the road she pulled into the grocery parking lot and cried. She had no idea how long she was there.

An older man knocked on her window. "Are you okay?"

Shaking her head, she wiped her nose and eyes. She watched him walk away and then opened up her glove box only to find some stiff napkins to wipe her face. She had to pull herself together for the drive home.

****

David stood looking out the window of Eric's apartment.

"You really are a dickhead. You know that, right?" Eric said dryly, putting his beer on the table. "She was the best thing that could have happened to you, and you threw her away."

"I didn't throw *us* away. She did." David turned around. "She was the one who returned the ring and ended it."

Eric snorted and shook his head, "Yes, but you drove her to it." He paused. "You invited Cathy to that cocktail party because you wanted to impress people. Hell, Jillian would've been a much better choice. She can easily carry on a conversation with anyone. And don't get me started on the difference in personalities."

"I know. You have to tell me where she's living."

"See? That's the other thing. The fact that you don't even know where she lives says a lot. She and Tara moved into their apartment a week after you left for Knoxville. I remember Jillian asking you to help them. Since you couldn't, they asked me."

Eric held his head to the side, crossing his arms. "It's Monday. This all happened on Friday night. If you really cared, then you would have gotten your ass up here *on* Friday night."

"She told me not to follow her."

"Girls say that. But if you care, you follow. And you grovel all weekend to win her back. She might have listened."

"I had twelve-hour shifts on Saturday and Sunday," David replied. Looking at Eric again, he demanded, "Tell me where she lives."

"Listen, I was over there on Saturday morning. Before I left, they said they would castrate me if I told you where they lived."

"Give me a break. I forget their address."

Eric shook his head. "Forgot it? Really? It wasn't lost on anyone that you never came up to see Jillian. Do you even know the name of the school she teaches at?'

David knew then, he wasn't going to win. "No," he whispered.

"Sad," Eric said pithily. "Your life revolved around you and your career. You didn't try to find out one thing about hers. Why did you love her? Because she was beautiful, and a model?"

"Shut up. That's not true at all," David said angrily.

"She knew everything about you, and you knew so little about her."

David stood digesting these words, not wanting to acknowledge their truth. He dropped onto the couch. Propping his elbows on his knees, he buried his head in his hands. He was an asshole, with a capital A. "How do I get her back, if she won't see me?"

"As your friend, I could call her."

"Do it," David replied quickly.

He watched Eric pick up the phone to dial her number.

David had left her at least twenty messages by now.

"Hey Tara, it's Eric. Is Jillian there?" Eric tapped his foot while he waited. "Jillian, how are you doing?"

Through the receiver David could hear Jillian's voice but couldn't make out the words.

"Well, that's why I'm calling. He's sitting right here, looking like shit. Do you want to talk to him?" Another pause. Eric handed the phone to David.

"What do you want?" Jillian asked.

"I need to see you. We have to talk."

"You waited long enough."

Contritely, David said, "You told me you didn't want to see me."

"That's right. I don't. We are through David. You're free to be with Cathy, or whomever else you want to be with."

"I want to be with you."

"Not happening. I told you I didn't want her visiting you, and you still had her up. And to top it off, you lied. She didn't know anything about our engagement."

"I told her."

"You did? Based upon the way you answered her when she asked, I don't believe you. I didn't trust her, and now I can't trust you."

"Jillian," he begged her, "let's meet. I can't do this on the phone."

"Goodbye, David." She hung up the phone.

It was official. She was gone.

After every visit she'd made to Knoxville, he'd felt an emptiness inside when she left on Sundays. That was nothing compared to the hollowness he felt now.

He had never cried out when his father had beaten him. But he wanted to now.

****

David sat outside Nana and Grandpa's house. This was his last resort.

He had continued to call and leave messages for Jillian until the day the recording said the phone number no long existed.

He looked at the blue Victorian house, remembering the time right before graduation when he and Jillian had house sat. She'd said they were going to live in this the house, with lots of children, one day. This house not only contained her best childhood memories, but it was also therapeutic. It was where she'd lived when her mother passed. This was the place she came to last spring when Cathy had spewed lies to her about him. It was only reasonable to believe she was here now.

Garland was wrapped around the porch's rail. Lights were hung on the bushes in the front. Slowly, he walked up the steps, careful not to slip on the ice that had formed from the freezing rain.

Hesitantly, he knocked on the front door. Grandpa Sean opened the door.

"Mr. O'Malley," David said. "May I come in?"

"Who is it?" Nana walked into the front room. Seeing him, she said, "I was wondering when you were going to come and see me. Come in."

"Thank you, ma'am."

"Don't call me that. Makes me feel old," she said, smiling. "Do you want something to drink? It's cold and nasty out there."

"I'm fine, thank you."

"Come, sit in here." She pointed to where a wood fire was burning.

David sat on the lone chair near the fireplace wanting to shake this coldness he felt inside. "I know I'm probably the last person you want to see, but I need to talk to Jillian."

"If you came here even a month ago, I would've given you a good piece of my mind and probably clocked you one," Nana said.

Sean interjected, "I want to give you a piece of my mind now."

Nana looked at her husband. "Stop that. Let's hear him out."

Sean grumbled and sat on the love seat across from him.

"How is she?" David asked.

"She's still hurting, but is doing better. I believe time heals all wounds," she said softly.

If he looked only at her green eyes, he could see Jillian in them. They filled the room with warmth and compassion.

"I came here because I want to see her and apologize. I know I made a huge mistake—"

"You can say that again," Sean scolded.

Nana looked severely at him. "Enough from you."

She adjusted herself on the couch to focus on David before continuing. "She's not ready, David. Bless her heart, she's stubborn. She never got that from me." She turned to glare at Sean. "We've heard her side of the story. Now you tell us what happened."

David re-lived the painful scene that he had been playing over and over in his mind the last couple of months. He ended and looked at Jillian's grandparents.

"I know. I shoulda told Jillian about the party and had her come. I never should have invited Cathy. And I should have jumped in the car and followed Jillian home. I know now that I shouldn't have taken her at her word. She was in an emotional state. I wasn't thinking very clearly myself."

"Life is full of regrets and 'shoulda, woulda, couldas,'" Nana said. "There is no rewind button in life. We need to learn from and not make the same mistakes again."

"That is what I'm trying to do. I love Jillian. She is the only one for me. Nothing happened between Cathy and me, nor would it ever." He looked at the floor and raked his hands through his hair.

Looking back up, he continued, "I want to tell her I love her and beg for her forgiveness."

Nana studied him. "I believe you, David. I do."

"Can you help me then?"

"I will talk to her—"

Sean interrupted, "You can't mean that."

"Let me finish..." she said. "I will talk to her. I hate it when two people who are so in love and so right for each other, like you two, are separated. But David, I think she's going to need more time."

His heart sank.

"Here's the thing... Jillian is beautiful and smart." With a knowing look in her bright green eyes, she said, "I know you were her first. I was even worried at how fast she fell for you. Part of me thought she needed to spread her wings a little more. But she and Tara both reminded me how much of the world she had experienced already." She paused. "Am I making a sense?"

"Not really," David said truthfully.

"Okay, let me try this. Excuse the cliché, but sometimes we don't know what we had until it's gone. I think that's where you and Jillian are. I think you know, but I'm not sure she does. Heck, Sean didn't when we were dating."

"Why are you bringing that up?" her husband huffed.

Nana sat back regally. "Because it was a defining moment for us, just as this is for David and Jillian. You were a prime example that men don't develop common sense until they're in their forties."

"What happened?" David asked sitting back.

"We were dating, seriously, and I was expecting to get a marriage proposal any day. Then one day, I saw him driving down the street with a beautiful girl in his car. He goes two weeks without calling me or stopping by the house. I walk into the ice cream parlor with my friends, and there he is…with her. Some guy sat down and was yakking with us, and Ol' Mr. Jealousy, here, came right up and asked me to join him and the girl he was with."

Intrigued, David asked, "Who was the girl?"

"My cousin from Ireland," Sean says. He pointed to Nana. "She was mad I didn't tell her and introduce her to Margaret."

"He should have," Nana said. "See? Every male makes at least one bone-headed mistake in their life. And you made yours."

"Nana. I hate all this. Help me fix it," he pleaded.

"Do me a favor, Sean. Get me a piece of paper and write our address on it."

David had hoped for Jillian's address so he could camp at her place.

As though sensing what he was thinking, Nana shook her head. "She and Tara are skiing in Tahoe this week. Get some sleep and tomorrow write her a letter. Tell her what you just told us. I'll talk with her and give her the letter."

His stomach, along with any hope he had, plummeted into the bowels of the Earth.

"You see, you are young and you think you have all this time in the world. But you don't. One day you'll wake up and this older face, with wrinkles mind you, is looking back at you from the mirror. Life happens fast. You can't waste it with regrets."

David and Nana stood when Sean returned with the slip of paper.

"And I'll tell her those same words, too," Nana

said. Walking up to David, she placed her hand on his upper arm. "I can see from your eyes, you're in pain. Things will work out. You'll see. I expect in a few months, you'll be back together and this will all be in the past."

"I hope so." He walked to the door. "Thank you for everything."

Nana hugged him.

Stepping back out into the cold night, David hoped Nana was right. It was all he could wish for at this point.

Chapter 18

Current Day

Stepping from the patient-transport elevator, David saw Jillian's parents and Tara in the waiting area. Even with the passing years, he could spot them anywhere. He stood off to the side to allow others from the hospital staff past. From his spot near the nursing station, he could observe them without being seen.

Barb and Patrick sat in two chairs, holding hands. Both looked tired and worried. The blonde pacing in front of the windows was obviously Tara. She still had the same walk. Her hair was long and thick, as it was the last time he'd seen her—when he had proposed to Jillian.

Sitting next to Barb was a tall, slender man with glasses. He stood up in front of Tara, seemingly to say something. Tara shook her head and leaned into the man. The man was probably Tara's husband but could be Jillian's. David had seen from the chart that her last name was now Taylor.

"Are you spying?" Eric startled him.

"I guess so. After all these years, I'm not sure how they would react to seeing me," David said.

The silence he had received after the letter he'd written had spoken volumes. She hadn't wanted to see him.

"Do you know how she is?" David asked Eric.

"She's still in surgery. Collapsed lung, broken wrist. Good news is the internal bleeding has been stopped and the pressure in her brain relieved. She took a hard hit."

David closed his eyes, not wanting to picture her in this condition. Inhaling deeply, he nodded his head in acknowledgement.

"There is something else. When we pulled up her electronic record, she has had breast cancer." Eric paused. "Twice."

That knocked the air from David. "Omigawd," he croaked. He looked to the man standing by Tara. *Please don't let that be her husband.* "Her mother died from breast cancer," he said quietly.

Eric nodded. "I'm going over. They were our friends. I think you should come, too."

"In a minute," David answered.

"Fine." Eric walked to the waiting area.

Tara immediately turned toward him. Her hand went to her mouth, looking as if she was seeing a ghost. There was no mistaking the tears in her eyes.

Eric squatted in front of Barb and Patrick. Soon the three were standing, and Tara joined them. He turned his head and said something to her. Demur smiles were on all their faces.

Tara introduced the man standing next to her to Eric. Hands were shaken. Now David wished he had followed Eric so he could know what they were saying to each other. They appeared to hang on every word Eric said.

Without warning, Tara's eyes latched onto David's. Slowly, she walked toward him. He wasn't able to decipher her sad expression. Her pace quickened until she was right in front of him. He was completely taken aback when she wrapped her arms around him to squeeze tightly. Hesitantly, he hugged her back.

"I can't believe it's you," she whispered. Her tears were wet against his neck. She finally released her grasp and took a step away to look him up and down.

He smiled meekly. "I was worried, when you quickened your pace that I was going to be the recipient of another shiner. I remember your right hook."

"That was in the past." Her voice was still husky. "Why are you standing over here?"

"I didn't know if any of you were ready to see me—considering how things ended."

She glanced up at the ceiling before looking back to him. "That was a long time ago, too long if you ask me. So much has happened since then, David."

Tara rested her hand on his upper arm. "If it was up to me—and if anyone listened to me—things would have been different. But that's a discussion for another day."

She sounded grown-up and mature, so unlike the carefree, fun-loving Tara he remembered. What had changed her?

"Come," she said gently, tugging on his shirt sleeve. "Come say hello to everyone. I have someone I want you to meet."

David followed her, trying to mask his limp.

Tara looked at him questioningly out of the corner of her eye but remained quiet, walking alongside him to join the others.

Eric stepped aside to allow him to shake hands with Patrick and Barb.

He felt Tara and Eric watching his every move.

She stood next to the tall man. "David, this is my husband, Peter. Peter, this is David Rainer. The same David that was with Jillian a long time ago."

So they talked about him?

Peter extended his hand to shake David's. It was a firm grasp. "Pleasure to meet you."

"Same here," David said. "Wish it was under better circumstances though."

Barb gasped. "Don't say it that way, David. She'll pull through."

Tara smiled. "That's for sure. She's a fighter and has never given up." She leveled her eyes on him. There was some inner meaning to those words. Was it the cancer?

Before David could ask what she meant, Eric was pulling his vibrating phone from his pocket. Looking at the screen, he said, "It's Lynda. I've got to take this. I was supposed to be home by seven, and it's now later than that."

In silence, the group watched him walk away.

"Lynda?" Barb asked.

"His wife," David and Tara said, at the same time.

So Tara knew he was married.

"She volunteers at Vickery Elementary," Tara admitted. "Jillian and I figured out who she was. She didn't know that we knew her husband."

There was a lightheartedness in Tara's face that brought back memories of their youth. She gestured to the chairs for them to sit.

"There was this one time—we were decorating the school for the spring festival. Lynda was complaining about something Eric had done. I started asking questions. Well Jilly overheard and immediately came to silence me in her teacher-like way." Tara snorted. "I know she was just as curious as I was, but it was a time when she wasn't feeling or looking her best. She was painfully thin, and her hair wasn't growing back as fast as mine."

"As yours?"

"Yep. We all shaved our hair to bolster her when she was going through chemo."

"We?" David looked incredulously at Tara.

"Me, Peter, Barb, and our friend Carol. Our daughter Emily wanted to, but Jillian wouldn't hear of it, so she got a pixie cut instead. It was to show our support for what she was having to deal with. I mean it was just hair and would grow back. It was the least we could do."

David was stunned at the extent of their friendship.

"Carol, who works for the paper, wrote a story about it because we were donating our hair for Wigs for Cancer Patients. The article generated a lot of publicity, and the salons near us set up a day for free cuts if you donated your hair for the cause."

David remembered seeing something about that in the paper. He'd not read the whole article so never knew it had ties to Jillian.

"So enough about that. What do you know about how Jillian is doing in surgery?"

He looked back at the double doors behind the station. "I don't have any details."

Barb and Patrick said nothing, but he could tell they were expecting him to do something.

"Let me see what I can find out." He limped toward the surgical doors. Damned rainy weather always made his lameness more pronounced.

Just as he rounded the station and opened the door, surgeon Carl Robertson leaned toward the desk. "Which is the family for Mrs. Taylor?"

The nurse pointed toward Tara and the O'Malleys. Dr. Robertson strode over to the family to talk with them.

David could tell, from the looks on the relieved faces, Carl was delivering good news. Those were tears of joy. Tara looked over at him and flashed a thumbs up sign.

Carl walked back in David's direction. "Rainer. A surprise to see you up here. Didn't know you had a surgery scheduled this late."

"I don't. I was actually checking on Jillian Taylor. I'm friends with the family."

Carl said, "It was touch-and-go for a while. She lost a lot of blood. She's stable, but we've put her in an induced coma for a few days."

"Thanks," David said.

"Hey, what do you know about a Dr. Cathy Barone? I heard she's a friend of yours."

"We were in medical school together here at UK. Why?"

Carl was about to speak when Tara appeared at his side. "I don't mean to interrupt," she said.

Carl looked at David. "Let's chat about this later."

David, with a sinking feeling, watched him walk away before focusing his attention on Tara.

"Peter and I are taking Barb and Patrick home. They're still in shock," she said gently. "Here's my number. We need to talk and catch up."

He took the card and gave her his number. She

programmed it into her phone. Standing on her tiptoes, she kissed him on his cheek.

"'Bye David. I'm glad you're back."

Chapter 19

David pulled up tomorrow's schedule to see if he had any planned procedures that would require a full night's sleep for him to be alert in the morning. There were none, only office consultations all day. He was also glad to see he was not on call until Saturday. He stayed at the hospital until Jillian was moved to an ICU room.

Eric had called to see if there were any updates. Once David filled him in, he decided to make his way to her room.

The ICU was a depressing part of the hospital with people in critical condition, some clinging to life. On this floor, voices were hushed and numerous monitors beeped. The only loud noises occurred when a team rushed to a bedside with lifesaving equipment.

Veronica, a mixture of compassion and no nonsense, was head nurse tonight. She comforted family members in their time of need, but other times had no trouble telling an arrogant doctor a thing or two.

From the very beginning, David showed her the respect she was due and was thus "one of her favorites." He knew some found this surprising as he'd heard through the grapevine how he was perceived.

Jillian's room was down the hall, away from the center desk.

He stood outside, watching her sleep.

Veronica appeared at his side. "Even with the facial bruising and the IV and monitor hookups, you can tell she's stunning. How come some woman age so gracefully?"

"I don't know." He considered what he must look like. *Would she recognize me?*

"What brings you here? I know she's not your patient since there's no heart issue."

"She's a friend," he said.

Veronica's sharp brown eyes looked at him. She walked away to check on other patients.

David went into Jillian's room and pushed the door so it was open only a crack, in case anyone needed to come inside. Standing at her bedside, he could do nothing but stare at the woman who was once to have been his wife.

He'd done a lot of thinking over the years. Eric had been right. His total self-involvement back then—only caring about his career and getting ahead—had been his intent when it should have been her.

It had taken several years for him to really come to terms with why she'd left. There were periods when he thought he had made peace with the outcome, only to have a subtle reminder of her make him relive those excruciating days.

Placing his hand over hers now, the memory of her touch and how she'd made him feel came flooding back. She made him happy and whole. Without her, there was no meaning to the word "love."

Even when he was with Margo for several years, he never felt content. When her interior design company had offered her a career advancement on the west coast, she'd told him that she sensed his heart belonged to someone else. The departure was amicable, and it made his decision to accept a position at University Hospital in Lexington easy.

And now, he was holding Jillian again, even if only her still hand. He pulled the chair closer so that he could sit and remain touching her. The surrounding monitors quietly hummed to the rhythm of her breathing.

What is she thinking? Can she feel me? Science had confirmed that people in comas could hear voices, but was she ready to hear his.

"I'm sorry, Jillian," he finally said, "for everything I did wrong. I was an idiot. I wanted to apologize and win you back, but you disappeared. I saved all the things you left at my place. I could never get rid of them, because in doing so, I would have been throwing you out. I now try to take a true interest in people, since I didn't do that with you. I think that was the lesson you were trying to teach me. And…I'm sorry for all the pain I inflicted on you through my ignorance." His rambling stopped when there was a sound outside the door.

Silently Veronica entered, carrying a pillow. Her kind eyes signaled she had heard at least part of what he had said. "I have to check her vitals. I also thought this would make you more comfortable."

"Thank you, Veronica." He made to stand to take the pillow from her.

"Don't get up, unless you need to stretch your legs." She went around the bed to where he sat. "You know that chair reclines."

He looked over the side to find the handle he hadn't been aware of.

Veronica checked the monitors and typed in a few things on the tablet she carried. "She's doing well." She smiled at him. "I think she knows you're here. There were a few blips in her heart rate in the last few minutes. I'll be back in a little bit to check on both of you."

"Thanks, Veronica."

She nodded before walking over to shut the blinds. Quietly, she left the room, closing the door completely behind her.

Leaning the chair back, David adjusted the pillow to be able to watch Jillian sleep as he held her hand.

Chapter 20

David pulled in front of Tara's house in Vickery. Ironically it was not even five minutes from Eric and Lynda's. The modest, yet elegant brick house's outside lights reflected up the walls. The landscaping was impeccable.

Upon pressing the doorbell, he heard voices, footsteps, and a barking dog.

Peter answered the door, saying, "Welcome to our mayhem."

A familiar-looking teenager held the collar of a springer spaniel. "This is Kyle," Peter said to David. "Kyle, this is Dr. David Rainer. He went to school with your mom and Aunt Jillian."

"Pleased to meet you," said Kyle, shaking his hand.

Tara walked into the foyer from the back of the house. "Let Juno outside, so she doesn't bother our guest."

The dog ran outside as soon as Kyle opened the door.

David took a good, long look at Tara in her jeans and blouse. Remembering how she had struggled with her weight, he thought she seemed to have landed at an average size—neither slim nor overweight. She tucked a strand of her shoulder-length thick, wavy blonde hair behind her ear. Her face seemed more relaxed than it did last night. Returned was a flash of spunk in her eyes.

David handed the bottle of Pinot Noir he'd picked up to Tara. "I remember you and Jillian drinking wine. Hope you like this."

"Thank you." Tara took the bottle from him.

"Did you have any trouble finding the house?" Peter asked.

"No. As it happens, I frequent your neighborhood. Eric and his wife live down the street in McClure Country Club."

"Yes, we knew that." Tara turned to head back where she came from. "Do you want anything to drink? Beer, wine, bourbon?"

"Water will be fine." David followed her, with Peter behind him.

"Suit yourself, but I think you're going to need something stronger." She proceeded to open the wine he'd brought. She filled a glass of water from the dispenser in the fridge for him "Let's go sit on the screen porch," she said.

Peter also poured himself a glass of wine. "I'll be in here watching the news. Let me know if you need anything."

Tara opened the back door to the porch.

Her decorating style should be featured in a magazine. David took the chair with the ottoman and she sat caddy-corner to him in the love seat.

"So tell me, David, what happened to you?" she asked softly.

"I thought you were going to tell me about Jillian. My past is—"

"Your past is part of this, and I won't start until you tell me what happened with your leg."

"It's actually my hip—a skiing accident in Colorado. In college, you and Jillian skied. I decided to learn—in case we ever got back together."

Tara took a sip, then rested the glass in her hands on her lap. "How long have you been back in Lexington?"

"Three years."

Tara said nothing, signaling for him to continue.

He didn't want to talk about this life. He was here to find out about Jillian's.

"After Knoxville, I moved to Atlanta. And before you say anything, it wasn't for Cathy. Though she did open a door for me to join a cardiology group there."

"I'm sure there was no ulterior motive on her part."

"At one time, she had wanted to be a cardiologist. You may actually find this surprising—she doesn't have the best bedside manners and was told this on more than one occasion. She ended up as an anesthesiologist.

"Probably suits her."

"When I moved to Atlanta, she was dating someone. They actually did get married."

"Someone married her?"

He nodded his head. "Didn't last."

"Shocker!" Tara said.

"Enough about me. When we talked earlier, I said I wanted to know about Jillian. I need to know what you meant yesterday when you said if it was up to you, things would have turned out differently."

Tara took a big sip of wine. "When Jilly came home from your apartment that night, I immediately knew something was up. She told us what happened. You know me—I immediately wanted to get in the car and do bodily harm to you and that evil bitch. I was ready to, but Peter stopped me. Jillian said her last image of you was you standing in the parking lot with slumped shoulders."

"She told me not to follow or call her," David said.

Tara shook her head. "When will the male species learn? Sometimes our words don't match what we want."

"And you want to know why we get confused."

"I'll give you that."

Tara sipped her wine and set it on the table next to her. "I left Eric a message asking if he'd heard from you, and to call. We left the message so late, he knew something was up, and came over the next morning after the end of his shift. He was livid when he heard. It was then Jillian brought up that you wouldn't come since you'd never been to our apartment. She was right, of course, you probably had no idea where we lived. We told Eric he couldn't tell you. Jillian made it abundantly clear she needed time to think and sort everything out."

"What did she need to think about? Gawd, I loved her."

"You see, whether right or wrong, she felt like the love was one-sided, and she was doing all the work to keep it going."

She paused. "David, you could've made more time for her."

"I know. I was wrong," he said dejectedly. He bent forward to put his elbows on his knees. "Looking back, I was pretty selfish then."

Tara's momentary silence signaled her agreement. "She was, too. And after a few months, I told her so.

She should've met with you in a neutral location and worked it out. Both Nana and I tried to convince her she was being stubborn. Nana told us about your visit and how lost you looked. She said no actor could pull off the pain she saw in your eyes."

Tara reached over to touch his knee. "I read the letter. It was beautiful. I told her to call you, but by then she felt it was too late. She said she'd look weak crawling back to you. She had convinced herself it was only a matter of time before it, or something like it, happened again."

"It wouldn't have," David quickly said. "I just can't believe that's how Jillian perceived our relationship. Why did she think it was too late?"

Tara sat back regarding him. "It probably wasn't, initially. But the letter arrived at the same time Nana came down with pneumonia, and then Grandpa had a heart attack."

"Oh, no."

"It was almost three months after its postmark that we finally read it. By then Jillian had accepted a teaching position at a private school in Louisville. Her contract was for three years, and it had a pretty stiff termination clause."

"I thought she'd never move away from here."

"Neither did I! I was pretty devastated too. We were best friends and the person I had basically lived with for the previous five years. She moved right before school started. It was hard on both of us."

David knew how close the two were. "What did you do?"

"Our friend Carol moved in, but it wasn't the same. I walked around in a trance for a while. I felt like I'd lost too many friends. Thank goodness for Peter."

"What do you mean, 'lost too many friends'?" David picked up his water for a drink.

"Once we got back from skiing, we started seeing less and less of Eric. He had a girlfriend who didn't like us. Plus, Eric reminded us of you, and what we all had together. Eric would always bring you up, and Jillian didn't want to hear about any of that."

"Really?"

"Yes, I think he was trying to get you two back together. Anyway, a year after Jillian moved out, Peter and I got engaged and obviously got married. Jillian was my maid of honor—the best ever. She catered to every need and never lost her cool, even when I did become a bridezilla."

David chuckled. He could easily picture Tara throwing tantrums and Jillian playing peacemaker.

"She brought a date with her to the wedding— Brian Taylor, a pilot for an overnight packages delivery company. His company had leased a few apartments, for their pilots' use during layovers, in the same complex where Jillian lived. He was several years older but completely head-over-heels for her. He transferred his home base to Louisville just to be near her."

Tara took another sip of her wine. There was less than an ounce left. She swirled the liquid before finishing it and putting her empty glass down. "He was so in love with her, but she didn't love him back to the same degree. She didn't have the same look in her eyes she had with you."

"I think she settled," Peter said, coming onto the porch. He turned on the heat lamp. He had the bottle of wine and an extra glass with him. Tara held out her glass, which he filled halfway. "Would you care to join my darling wife?" Peter poured him a glass after David nodded.

"Thank you," David said. "So you think she settled?"

"Oh yeah. The only person who didn't see that was Brian," Peter said. "Nice guy. She seemed content enough, but it was as though she was holding something back." He shrugged his shoulders. "Just my observation."

He bent to kiss his wife. "I'm going to pick Emily up."

"Emily?" David asked.

"She's Kyle's twin. She's over at friend's, studying for a midterm exam. They can't wait to get their licenses so they can drive without us being in the car. Only one more month before that happens."

Once again, Tara and David were alone on the porch. She didn't touch her wine. "It took a while, but Jillian finally had a child. Danny. He was a beautiful child, inside and out. He took the best of both of them. She was finally happy, considering all the miscarriages she'd had."

Tara reached for a manila envelope on the table that David hadn't noticed. Pulling out a photo, she looked at it before handing to him. "Here's a picture of them."

His insides tightened when he looked at the picture of Jillian and her son. He certainly had her eyes, black hair, and slender face but missing were her Native American features including the complexion. He had a smattering of freckles across his nose. She looked joyous.

Tara took the picture back from him and returned it to the envelope.

"When Danny was two, she wanted to have another. Brian worried over the difficult pregnancy she'd had. At her annual visit, instead of talking about more babies, she and her doctor discussed the lump they found in her breast. She had stage II breast cancer. It was a big tumor, but thankfully it hadn't spread to her lymph nodes yet."

"Omigawd."

"Brian had crazy hours and couldn't always be there for her. He was a wreck. Gawd love him. Peter and I, and her parents were her main support system. It was a long and painful process. The hardest was the chemo. After her third cancer-free anniversary they decided to move here. I, for one, was over the moon."

David smiled. "I'm sure you were."

"They were going to move into Nana's house to be with her. Grandpa had died a few months before from a second heart attack. A month before they were to move, Nana passed away in her sleep."

"I'm sorry."

"It was hard on Jillian. She kicked herself for not moving earlier to be there for Nana. She said 'nothing would have happened to Brian or Danny, either, if we'd been here.' You see, we'd all tried to assure her they were just in the wrong place at the wrong time."

David was perplexed, "I don't understand."

"Let me back up. Before they could move back, Jillian needed to finish out the school year as assistant principal at the school in Louisville."

Tara turned her face to the side, and David saw her suck in her bottom lip. "The day after school ended,

Jillian drove out here early in the morning to meet with Vickery Elementary's outgoing principal. Danny wanted to come with her, but Jillian told him he'd be coming later that evening with his dad. It would give him a chance to spend one last day with his friends." Tara's voice had begun quivering.

David reached for her clenched hand.

"They never made it—hit by a drunk driver. It was four o'clock in the afternoon, and the guy was beyond drunk. He had no recollection of the accident. It was his third DUI. Brian and Danny were killed on impact." Tara's tears were flowing.

David moved to the couch to put his arm around her.

She leaned against him. "He was only seven years old." Tara wiped the tears from her eyes. "Jillian was, of course, a mess. Within months, she'd lost the grandparents who were everything to her, her son, and her husband. There were times that Barb, Carol, and I would visit, and she'd just be sitting in a daze."

Tara swiped at her cheeks again. "We reminded her that Danny was in heaven with Nana, Grandpa, Brian, and her mom. They were all looking down on her. At one point it was so bad, I suggested calling Eric to find you. I knew if I couldn't get through to her, then maybe you could."

Tara stood suddenly. "I'll be right back."

"I wished you had," he said to her retreating back.

Tara stopped but didn't turn around, "Barb and Carol wouldn't let me."

Tara walked inside to blow her nose.

As hard as it was to hear Jillian had been married with a child that should have been his, it was tougher to learn of their deaths. David picked up the glass of wine, wishing, as Tara had suggested, it was something stronger and took a gulp. He wished she had made the call.

"Sorry about that," Tara said, returning with a box of tissues. "Emily and Kyle were eleven at the time and I remember hugging them so close. It was then that I became a helicopter mom. As a mother I couldn't bear the thought of losing a child. I remember Jillian once saying everything she loved had been taken from her." Tara stopped.

The meaning was not lost on David.

"Thankfully, she was living here, and all of us were there for her. She pulled herself together. Life slowly became tolerable and livable again. With all her focus on healing her broken heart and settling into the new school as principal, she unfortunately overlooked taking care of herself. A year later, at a follow-up visit, she had a mammogram."

David leaned back and ran his fingers through his hair. He knew what this meant.

"This time it was Stage III and had traveled to the lymph nodes. We only *thought* it was a difficult road before. This was longer and harder. The chemo made Jillian sicker this time, and she lost so much weight. There were times I thought she would just give up."

Tara sniffled and blew her nose again. "She had the support of the community behind her though. The one thorn in this was Parent Booster Club President Shannon Bauer. She called for Jillian's resignation. According to her, 'the school and the taxpayers deserved a better principal than the damaged goods that they received.' Those were her exact words."

"Are you kidding me?" David asked incredulously.

"Yep. Our friend Carol did some research and learned Shannon's cousin was passed over for the principal's position. The good news was the public outpouring in support of Jillian was incredible. Everyone, including Jillian, worked to raise awareness. She was the poster child in this area for breast cancer. There were pictures of her at rallies and walks, with her signature blue-and-white UK silk scarf covering her bald head."

Tara pulled out two pictures of Jillian. Her face gaunt, she was incredibly thin. One showed her flanked by Peter and Tara as she walked. The other had her surrounded by a bunch of school-aged children, all wearing pink shirts.

"Her goal is to make it to the five-year cancer-free mark."

She inhaled deeply. "So that is the briefest summary I can give you on Jilly's life."

Tara closed her eyes and leaned her head against the cushions. "You spent the night in her room, didn't you?" she asked.

"How did you know?"

"I just did. I knew when I saw you at the hospital yesterday that you would. I could see that you still care for her."

Tara sat up straight in the love seat and angled her body to face him. "She's had more than her fair share of pain and loss. She can't take any more."

"I hear you. I don't want to be the cause of anymore."

Tara took his hand. "Be there for her. And don't make me get mad with you."

"Got it," he said solemnly.

Leaving, David felt drained. It had been a long evening, but he needed to know. It pained him to hear the story, but he had a better understanding of Jillian, past and present.

Typical of Tara, she never held anything back, including her threat of bodily harm if he hurt her friend again.

Chapter 21

Her eyes felt heavy. Jillian tried to open them, but they would not move. It felt as if she had had too much to drink. There was a humming noise followed by some beeps. Someone was saying her name. It sounded both low and far away.

She tried to open her eyes again, but they wouldn't budge. Were they glued together? Panic set in.

What's wrong? What's happening to me? her mind screamed. She felt herself breathing heavily. Her chest was constricted. *Is somebody sitting on me? Is it Shadow? That cat is too damned fat.* She could feel her pulse quicken, and it pounded in her ears. It was loud, and it hurt her head.

She tried to open her mouth to scream, but nothing happened. *Omigod,* she thought, *I am dead. Danny! Nana! Where are you? It's me. I'm here. Where are you? I can't see you.* Her mind stopped.

Her head felt as if it weighed a ton. She wished whoever was saying her name would stop. She wanted to tell them to leave.

She tried to move and felt a sharp pain in her chest. She wasn't sure if she moaned. The voices continued to chatter. Soon it was quiet except for the humming/intermittent beeping noises. Maybe the beep was her alarm clock. She tried to lift her hand to turn it off, but she couldn't.

"Jillian? Can you hear me?" asked a deep voice.

She wanted to hear that voice. It was comforting. There was a gentle grip on her hand, and he repeated her name. Immediately the beeping sounds increased in number and volume. The rush of voices started again.

She was so tired. Her mind told her not to fight. Why was she so sleepy? She let the warm feeling engulf her and drifted back into darkness.

****

"Jillian? Jillian, can you hear me?" a male voice said.

She opened her eyes, blinking several times. The room seemed too bright.

A very dark-eyed man's face loomed in front of her. Next to his, was an older woman's face.

"Jillian. Nice to see you," he said. "How are you feeling?"

"Tired. It hurts to move."

He nodded his head before shining a bright light in each of her eyes.

"Are you a doctor?" She shut her eyes against the light. "My chest hurts."

"You're going to be sore. On a scale of one to ten, how would you rate the pain? One being no pain and ten being excruciating."

"A five."

"Do you know where you are?" the man asked.

Without lifting her head, she glanced around. "A hospital," she answered. Her lips were dry. "I remember a truck coming through the intersection. He was supposed to stop."

"That's right. You're one lucky lady. I'm Dr. Cole. Dr. Robertson, your surgeon, and Dr. Brody, your oncologist have been checking on you here in the ICU. You've had a contingent of folks keeping vigil in the waiting room."

She licked her dry lips.

"Can you send in Tara and my dad?"

"Sure, but just for a few minutes. You need your rest, and I don't want you overdoing it."

She nodded. Her throat was so dry.

He left the room, and the nurse ushered in her best friend and her father. Both had tears in their eyes.

"You have fifteen minutes. That's all," said the nurse.

"I'm so happy you're okay," her dad said. He leaned over to kiss her forehead and held her hand.

"We all are," Tara said. "You do know you're the one who makes me have to color the gray out of my hair."

"You bring it on yourself." Jillian smiled weakly. "I meant to call you yesterday to say I was running late. But you know me—I can't manage an umbrella and phone at the same time."

"Yesterday?" Tara asked.

"Yeah, yesterday…after my monthly meeting with the superintendent."

Her father spoke. "Jillian, it's Saturday afternoon. Your appointment was on Wednesday."

Jillian blinked at the two of them. Tara nodded in agreement.

Tara sat on the edge of the bed. "You've been in a coma for a couple days, due to head and internal injuries."

Dad continued to stand.

"You'll never guess who the doctor was in the

ER," Tara said. "Eric. Eric Laughlin."

"Really?"

Nodding, Tara's eyes darted between her and her dad. There was something else.

"David was there, too. He saw you."

Jillian was speechless. She looked to her father who confirmed.

"We talked with him that evening when you were in surgery," he said.

"Jilly, I think he's been sleeping in your room. He wouldn't confirm or deny when I asked him," Tara said.

All eyes were on Tara.

"He came to my house on Thursday evening. We had a nice little chat," Tara added.

"You talked with him? At your house?"

"Yeah. Oh Jillian, if you could see him. He looks so unhappy."

"What did you tell him?" Jillian asked nervously.

"Um…let's see…"

"Tara!"

"I, uh…told him, uh… He wanted to know what happened since *that night*. I told him, and he…well he knows about Danny and Brian."

"What?" she exclaimed.

"Jillian, calm down. I couldn't help it. He wanted to know. And you know me, once I start, I can't stop. Of course, I blubbered like an idiot at the sad parts. I probably went through half a box of tissues. I'm sure I gave myself a few more wrinkles."

"Serves you right. Why did you tell him?"

Tara let out a big sigh. "Because he asked."

Dad interjected. "Jillian, he seemed genuinely

concerned that night you were in surgery."

She looked to her dad's clear eyes.

"I think he still cares for you," he added.

"There's more," Tara added.

As if this couldn't get any worse. Jillian sighed, waiting to hear.

"He's changed. He looks much older than he is. He's had an accident and has a hitch in his giddy-up."

Jillian closed her eyes, trying to picture him. The day they walked in the park came to her clearly.

"He's still aloof, but there's a sense of compassion that I don't remember from before," Tara said. "When I saw him this morning, he said that since he wasn't there when you needed him before, that's he's here for you now."

Just as Jillian was about to respond, the nurse came in to say their time was up.

"Call me later," Tara said.

She nodded. It was time to put the hurt from the past aside.

Chapter 22

David finished making his cardiology rounds. He was also on call for heart patients coming through the Emergency Room. Throughout the entire day, Jillian had never been far from his thoughts. He'd slept at home last night, needing to be well-rested for today's early hospital hours.

Before starting rounds, he had checked on Jillian. Her chart showed there had been activity and movement late yesterday. Her accident report indicated that the car's airbags had deployed, but there was side whiplash, with her car being impacted with the front grill of the T-boning truck.

Stepping from the elevator, he nearly collided with Carl Robinson who was looking down at his phone.

Carl stopped abruptly. "Whoa, sorry about that. They say you shouldn't text and drive, but they never talk of the dangers of texting and walking."

"It's okay." David's sideways falter reminded him that by the end of the day, his hip would be throbbing. He'd skipped his morning swim.

"Hey, do you have a second to talk?" Carl asked. "I want to get your take on something."

"Sure." David followed him to the end of the hall, away from others.

Carl was tall and built like a runner. David missed those days.

Arms crossed, Carl said in a quiet voice, "There's no subtle way to ask this, so I'm just going to put it out there. What's the story with Dr. Cathy Barone?"

"What do you mean?" David leaned against the wall to take weight off his hip.

"I heard she's your friend, and you were the one who brought her up here…but seriously David, she—"

"I didn't recommend her." David was louder than he wanted to be. Lowering his voice, he continued, "In fact, I was surprised when she called to say she was moving…considering how much she hated it here."

Carl's eyes opened in surprise, "That isn't what she's saying. She alluding to…well, you know…that you're together."

"Not the case," David said harshly. His blood pressure rose.

"Oh." Carl rubbed one hand over his forehead and down his face. "This is embarrassing."

"Why?" David glanced down the hall at some passing staff.

"I was going to see if you could maybe talk to her about being a little more pleasant to the surgical staff. You know, not so condescending. None of the surgeons want her in the OR with them. None. In fact, she and Christy Leopald had it out yesterday. It was downright ugly. I would be surprised if Christy doesn't file a complaint."

"Seriously?"

"Yep. I told Jerry that I'd talk with you. As head of surgery, he's ready to go to Greg in Anesthesiology."

Shaking his head, David said, "If I run into her, I can try to talk with her."

"Well, sorry to bother you. I can see it's not really

your concern. By the way, your friend...Jillian Taylor..."

"Yes?" David discerned a quizzical look from Carl.

"I heard she's awake. They'll probably move her out of ICU once the neurologist clears her."

Without realizing it, David breathed a sigh of relief.

****

None of the food on the table-top tray looked even remotely appetizing. It was an ordeal for Jillian to lift her hand to pick up the fork and stab at the lettuce that was the salad—well, lettuce with a few slivers of carrot. Where were the spinach, cucumbers, and peppers? Her right shoulder throbbed, and she couldn't use her left hand as it was encased in a cast. To top it off, she was tired. Again.

Looking toward the windows where dusk was settling, she started to doze but then heard a noise.

"The food here isn't that good," a deep voice said.

She didn't have to turn her head to know the owner of that rich, velvety voice. A part of her was scared to look. Jillian knew this was not going to be the same person she'd known so many years ago, and yet her heart beat faster. She turned her head slowly toward the door. She wouldn't have recognized him, if Tara had not forewarned her of his presence.

She silently studied him. His dark hair still had that slight curl but was streaked with gray and was dull-looking. His face was etched with too many worry and frown lines. But it was his eyes that were most dismaying. They were still that intense blue, but instead of sparkling, they looked lifeless.

"It's been a long time, David. I hardly knew you

standing the door." Her lips twitched into a slight smile and she snapped her fingers. "Aren't those the words to a Neil Diamond song?"

His shoulders shrugged. "I don't know."

She cocked her head to the side and bit her lip. "I think it's *September Morn*. Don't you remember?"

"When it comes to Neil Diamond, I try to forget. You appear to have had a lapse in memory. You were the one who liked him, not me."

She cracked a smile, to lighten the tension in the room, "You're joking. You never said you didn't like him. You didn't complain when I played his cassette tape."

"I guess you didn't know I was hoping the player would eat your tapes."

"And ABBA? Did you pretend to like them, too?"

"I tolerated them. Their music made me laugh. Or maybe it was the way you and Tara imitated them—singing their songs at the top of your lungs."

"Fine. Say no more. Obviously, you don't have good taste in music," she said lightly. "Are you going to stay hovering by the door? I'm not going to attack you. In case you haven't noticed, I'm not exactly mobile. Come and sit down."

Gingerly, she moved her stiff legs to one side to allow him room to sit. She watched him limp to the chair. "What are you doing?" she asked.

"I'm sitting down."

Firmly, she said, "Listen, no doctor worth his grain of salt sits in a chair. They sit at the end of the bed. I've been around hospitals enough to know what makes a good doctor, and what doesn't." She pointed to the foot of the bed.

David moved slowly to the other side and sat with his right hip and leg on the bed.

"It's your left hip, that's injured, isn't it?"

He nodded.

"Tell me what happened."

"You don't want to hear it."

I do," Jillian said earnestly. "I want to know."

"The accident happened six years ago in Colorado. I had learned to ski, so if you and I ever got back together, we would have that it common."

"Really?"

"Yep. He looked away from her briefly. "Strangely enough, I was seeing someone else at the time. We were going down a rather steep slope. I lost control and slammed into a tree. Underwent extensive surgery to repair the hip bone and had months of physical therapy. They did the best job they could, but I knew I'd never walk normally again."

"What happened to the girl?" she asked.

"We went our separate ways. I was bitter and depressed. She was shallow—couldn't stand to see me naked anymore because of the scars and deformity in my hip."

"I'm sorry."

His sad eyes met here. "What are you sorry for? That I was doing something I enjoyed when a tree got in my way? Or that I walk with a pronounced limp on cold, rainy days because the surgeon did a crappy job?"

"I'm sorry for your hurt." Jillian took his large hand in hers. "Did you talk with a therapist about your depression?"

"No, I didn't. I thought it was a waste of time and wouldn't accomplish anything. It wasn't going to make me walk normally again."

"You don't know that it would have been a waste." She adjusted her bed to sit higher and winced when it went too high.

"Jillian, be careful," he said gently. He stood and helped to lower it. "How much does it hurt?"

"Right now it doesn't. That was just a quick stab."

After adjusting her pillow, David sat back on the bed but closer to her than previously. "You look good, Jillian. Age has been kind to you."

Apparently, he didn't want to talk about himself, nor his injury. "Like a fine wine, huh?" She smiled at him. "You look the same—just a little older and more tired. I suppose you still work long hours."

He nodded his head.

"Remember what Nana said about all work and no play? 'For your sake, don't miss out on your own life.'"

"I was sorry to hear about Nana. She was a good woman. You must miss her."

"I do." Changing the subject, Jillian asked, "Why did you move back to Lexington?"

"Eric told me about an open position. There were happy memories here. I wanted to come back."

"Where do you live now?"

"Over at Bridgewater."

"Wow. That's a real nice area. Good for you." She reached her right hand out to touch his face.

He bent forward a little to allow her.

Quietly she said, "You need to smile again," She left her hand on his cheek.

When she started to pull away, he grabbed it.

She looked at him with her hand in his. He rubbed his thumb over hers, and the old feeling returned.

A nurse came into the room, and Jillian immediately saw the look of surprise on her face at seeing David sitting on the bed, holding her hand.

David immediately pulled his hand free from hers.

The nurse mumbled something before leaving.

"I better get going before she has the whole hospital talking," David whispered.

"That would be bad, huh?"

"Yes, in the sense that doctors are not supposed to be fraternizing with attractive patients."

She smirked. "Oh but it's okay to fraternize with ugly ones? You forget. You're not my doctor, and I'm not your patient. Let them talk. Don't leave, David. Stay and talk with me. Tell me more about you. I already know you've heard everything about me from blabbermouth Tara."

Taking his hand again, she listened to him with the same fascination she'd had the first time they met.

Soon she wasn't just hearing his words, but became aware of the emotions the sound of his voice stirred up. Closing her eyes, she wanted to turn back the clock. Maybe they could forge ahead, to possibly rekindle what they'd had.

Chapter 23

The day was busier than expected with David filling in for a sick colleague. He had completed two angiograms on individuals who were too young to have heart conditions. These were the type of patients that made him regret letting life pass by as he had.

Hard to believe it was only a week since Jillian had re-entered his life. He stopped by when he could, both during the day and in the evening. She seemed to constantly have visitors. A few times, when there was no one, he was happy to see her resting. At those times, he would watch her sleep. He still had a concern on the hit she'd taken to the head.

She was different than he remembered—more confident. He supposed, among other things, that beating cancer twice played a role in this. He was around enough patients who looked at life differently when they'd been given a second chance.

Walking slowly down the hall toward the elevator, David rubbed at the tension in his neck. He would just gather his things before heading up to Jillian's room. The plan was for him to take her home.

"Hey, David, wait up," Cathy said, coming from a side hall.

Damn!

"Have you been ignoring my messages?" she asked loudly.

Yes.

When he didn't answer, she continued, "What's going on?"

"Been busy," he answered. He couldn't tell her the truth—at least not until he was on sure footing with Jillian. Then again, he didn't want to be around Cathy anyway.

"I'm done for the day. How about we grab dinner at that new restaurant that opened, Casa Nuevo?"

"Can't. I have plans." He started to walk to the elevators.

Following alongside, Cathy asked skeptically, "You do?"

"I do. Now if you'll excuse me, I'm late." He hit the button to summon the elevator.

Cathy's hands were on her hips. "You're seeing someone, aren't you?"

He paused. They weren't seeing each other, so he didn't need to answer to her. "Yes."

Cathy sighed before crossing her arms. Her steel eyes glared at him.

If looks could kill, I'd surely be dead.

Huffily she said, "I thought with me moving here, we could revive what we had."

"We never 'had' anything, Cathy. There was only ever friendship between us, except for what was in your imagination," he said gruffly. He stepped into the elevator.

Thankfully, she didn't follow. David rode the elevator up a floor to take the crosswalk to the medical building where his office was. He had to hurry to meet up with Jillian.

****

After this last week in the hospital, Jillian was ready to go home. The term "resting" was a joke. She was tired of people coming in and out at all hours. She was looking forward to sleeping in her own bed. She also missed her cat, Shadow.

That morning, she felt like she there had been a parade of physicians—the neurologist, the physical therapist, the surgeon, and her oncologist, Dr. Brody. Why he came she wasn't sure.

Earlier that morning her dad had dropped off her clothes. She sent him home with some of her flowers.

Tara couldn't get off work, since Jillian wasn't sure what time she was going to be discharged.

Barb had decided to clean the house for Jillian and do some grocery shopping. At least Barb knew what she ate. If her father had shopped, he would have bought none of what she liked, and all of what he ate.

With the discharge papers finally signed, she wondered who was taking her home. Neither Tara nor her dad was answering their phones. She was debating calling Carol when her door opened. Eric and a nurse were standing there.

"You aren't taking me home, are you?" Jillian asked, hesitantly.

"No. Tara asked if David wouldn't mind," Eric answered. "He's running a little late." He helped her into the wheelchair and picked up her bag. "He'll meet you downstairs."

"I'm so happy to be going home. Though I'm not saying I didn't enjoy this last week's little homecoming."

As the nurse pushed her down the hall, Eric replied. "I hope you are planning on taking it easy. You know you can call on me or Lynda anytime, right?"

She nodded. "Between my parents, Carol, Tara, and Peter checking on me all the time, I don't think I will have a moment's peace. I wouldn't be surprised if several of them haven't moved in already."

He chuckled. "In that case, it sounds like a party. I'll stop by, too. You know I'm not that far."

Outside, Jillian breathed in the cool, crisp autumn air. After her hospital confinement, she relished being outdoors, even in the evening air.

David opened the passenger door of a black Mercedes to help her in.

There was no mistaking the shock on the nurse's face as she looked first at David and then back to Jillian. Jillian had learned, from some of the nurses who cared for her that Dr. Rainer typically kept to himself. Though not unfriendly, he had the reputation of being standoffish and quiet.

Eric placed her bag in the back seat. He leaned down and looked at the car's two occupants. "See you around. And take good care of her," he said as he closed her door.

"Thank you for doing this, David. I hope I'm not inconveniencing you," she said. "Tara wasn't responding to any of my texts."

He briefly glanced over at her, "I don't mind at all."

"You can just drop me off. You probably had a busy day, and I'm sure you want to get home. Plus, Dad or Barb, if not both, will probably be at the house."

David was silent while he drove the luxury car through the traffic. She remembered his dad's sarcastic comment about him having a Mercedes.

At the next stop light, he angled his body toward her, "Jillian, I'm not just going to drop you off and leave. I want to make sure you're okay."

There was a slight flutter in her stomach. They had talked so much on that first night, and then she hardly saw him after that. It was as though he had been avoiding her.

She leaned to turn the radio on with her right hand.

He glanced at her, with a gentle smile. "You haven't changed, have you? Do you get in everyone's car and immediately put it on a station you want?"

"Yes, I still do that." She reached over and playfully slapped his arm before realizing hitting him with the cast on her wrist while he drove was probably a bad idea.

"Do you remember how to get there?"

"I do," he said.

After a few moments he continued. "When I moved back up here from Atlanta, I drove by Nana's once. There were two kids sitting on the porch. After seeing Tara's twins last week, I think it was them. If I had only stopped."

"Funny that we've been living so close and yet our paths never crossed," she said looking out at the dusk. Soon it would be Halloween. The days were getting shorter. Winter nights had been the hardest for her these past few years. She tried to keep busy, but at times the silence bothered her.

David came to a stop in front of the slate-blue Victorian house that she loved so much.

When she opened the car door, his hand was immediately on her left arm. "Wait, Jillian. Let me come around and help you."

Inwardly she smiled, wondering how *he* was going to help *her* walk. He opened the door and took her hand to assist her.

"I'll come out for the rest later," he said.

"David, no big deal. I can carry my bag. I am not completely inept." She was tired of being waited on as if she was an invalid.

"I'll get it." He reached into the back seat for her bag and pulled out a second one.

She raised one eyebrow.

"Barb and Tara made up the guest room for me. I'm spending the night to make sure you are okay. They like having a doctor at the house on your first night home."

"Oh, they do, do they? Glad you clarified." Jillian walked along the pathway to the front porch. "Guess they didn't want to give the impression I was easy."

As he unlocked the front door, she took in the sad fact that all her flowers on the porch were dead from lack of water. She would need to get rid of them.

The smell of cleaning assaulted her when she opened the door. Running down the stairs and meowing—or actually bellowing—at the top of her lungs was Shadow, her cat.

Jillian stepped around David to go inside. "Ah, so nice to be home."

Shadow tried to escape onto the porch. David quickly closed the door and looked around.

"I made a few changes." She rambled toward the kitchen in the back of the house, flipping on the lights as she went. "You can leave the bags on the stairs. I can take them up later."

"I'll take them up," he said.

She stopped, "Are you able to do stairs?"

"Yes," he said roughly.

"I'm sorry, I didn't mean it like that," she said apologetically.

David stood right behind her, and the air crackled with tension. The few times he visited in the hospital he had remained a respectable distance after that first incident with the nurse walking into the room. Here it was just the two of them with no possibility of interruptions.

His blue eyes looked into hers. Cupping her face in both his hands, he kissed her deeply in an effort to make up for twenty years. She kissed him back with the same fervent passion.

For the first time in all those years they were apart, Jillian felt her scalp tingle with excitement. She ran her hands up his chest and leaned into him. She could feel the beating of his heart matching hers.

His mouth felt so natural. They were one again. She was a sucker for him.

Smiling, she pulled him closer. She wanted to feel his mouth on the rest of her again.

Her phone chirped from her purse. It would be Tara, her parents, or Carol. *Nice timing.* Reaching into her purse, she said, "You know if I ignore it, they'll just keep calling. Or come over to make sure everything is okay."

"I know." He watched her intently.

It was her dad. She headed toward the door to the sunroom to talk. "Yes, Dad, I'm okay." Shadow appeared at her feet, weaving in and out, purring the entire time. "Yes, I know you're worried."

A few minutes later she hung up the phone and

went back into the house. David was no longer in the kitchen. She made her way to the front sitting room. He was standing rigidly, looking at her photos on the wall.

"I guess you can see I like pictures."

When he said nothing, she continued, "Are you hungry? I am sure there's plenty to eat."

"Sure," he replied. His demeanor was quiet.

Jillian returned to the kitchen and found the refrigerator stocked with food and beverages. She peeked inside the freezer—also stuffed. She started to laugh when she looked at the wine refrigerator and saw it, too, was full.

David moved slowly into the kitchen and asked, "What's so funny?"

"Barb and Dad not only did some grocery shopping, but also quite a bit of cooking. There's enough here for a year."

"So, what is there to eat?"

"It might be easier to answer what isn't here to eat." She rummaged through and found a container filled with soup. She opened the lid and smelled Barb's chicken soup. Barb, and Nana for that matter, thought chicken soup cured everything. It hadn't helped her broken heart twenty years ago.

Jillian put the soup on the stove. As she turned to get the loaf of bread sitting on the counter she bumped into him. "Sorry, I didn't know you were there."

His hands were on her arms. She had an urge to lean into him to kiss him again like they had earlier. He, however, didn't move. It felt as if he was now keeping her at a distance. She stepped to the side to grab the freshly baked bread.

They carried the heated food into the dining room.

Once seated, David said, "I like what you did to the house. It's very inviting."

"Thanks. Tara's always giving me pointers on what to do. Now her house—that's decorated. Everything looks just right. Mine is more, um…what's the word I'm searching for?" She stopped and looked at the ceiling. "Eclectic. That's it."

He took a spoonful of soup and looked around. "Eclectic?"

"Yeah. When I see something I like, I just buy it. I don't worry about if it matches or not. I make it fit in. I bought that bowl in the front foyer at a market in Spain. The table was from an antique store. See the picture on the wall over the buffet? I got that at an art show, in of all places, Switzerland."

Once finished eating, they brought their dishes to the kitchen. Jillian said, "Let's sit in the family room. It's pretty comfortable."

David walked around the room, taking in Jillian's taste in decor. He sat on the far corner of the couch.

She laughed as Shadow jumped up on the arm rest to inspect him. "I think she's checking you out. Either that or she's jealous. Her name is Shadow."

David rubbed the top of Shadow's head. "I didn't know you liked cats."

"It wasn't as if I hated cats. I just never had one. I know that is hard to believe, coming from the daughter of a vet. She was a gift from Emily and Kyle when I moved here. They didn't want me to be lonely. I called her Shadow because the first week she followed me everywhere. And I mean everywhere." She was now mindful that Shadow hadn't come to her and instead stayed by David's side.

"Tell me about you, David. All I've unearthed about your last twenty years is you learned to ski and now you live in Lexington."

"Well, I didn't learn to ski very well obviously. Other than that, there is nothing to tell." His voice sounding flat. "I think you need to turn in soon and get some sleep. It's been a busy day."

"I'm not ready, yet. I'm actually tired of being in bed."

****

David stared at Jillian. He had no idea where to start. The collage of pictures on her wall clearly demonstrated she had kept busy over the years. She'd fought cancer and hadn't let it beat her. What had he done? Compared to her—nothing.

For the first year after she left, going through the motions of daily living was it. One day he awoke realizing he needed to move on. Jillian was gone forever.

The most important thing to him became success at his job. He was quickly recognized for his work and there was the call from the cardiac group in Atlanta. It was his dream job, what he had been preparing for, and it was here.

He called his friends, except for Cathy, to let them know the news. She heard it through the grapevine. Though she was dating, she immediately inserted herself into his life—to help him with his move and introduce him to people.

They never spoke about the night Jillian had broken up with him. Soon Cathy broke it off with her boyfriend to actively pursue him. David had put her off more times than he could count. He started to date other woman, but Cathy never gave up—even after she married.

Jillian touched his arm. "David?" Her face studied his. "So I know you moved to Atlanta. How long did you live there?" she asked.

"About ten years." He watched the cat jump from the couch onto a chair by the window.

"Did you ever marry?"

He looked into her face. "No." *How can she even ask that?* His heart belonged to one woman. Yet, she'd had no problem marrying.

"Did you travel?" she asked.

"Not as much as you." He pushed himself to a standing position.

"Did I say something?" Jillian asked quietly.

He heard the tiredness in her voice. All he wanted was to take her in his arms and hold her. Yet, at the same time, he was angry—at himself for wasting twenty years of his life, and at her for living hers.

Looking again at the pictures, he asked, "Did you ever make it to Paris?"

"No," she said softly. "That was where you and I were to go. I couldn't bring myself to go there with Brian."

He glanced at her, and the resentment was gone. She had constantly talked about their honeymooning in Paris—the city of lovers.

"I told myself that when I hit five years of being cancer-free I was going to go."

"When is that?"

"End of November." Jillian ran her fingers through her long, dark hair. "But we'll have to wait until school gets out."

"We?" He was curious to know who the other person was.

"Tara, Peter, Emily, and Kyle are coming with me."

The tension slowly eased from his body. He returned to the couch to sit with Jillian.

Jillian's face took on an amused appearance. She turned to face him. "So…funny story… At one point Emily wanted to be a cheerleader. Never made it though, as she has this little problem of not following directions. Plus she likes being the center of things."

"Hmm, who does that sound like?"

"I know, right? Well, when I celebrated my second first cancer-free anniversary, Emily said I had to do a cartwheel since that is what you do to celebrate a win. So every year she and I do a cartwheel when I get the good news. I told them that for my fifth, however, I wanted to do something bigger."

"So you chose Paris?"

"Yep. Of course Emily says I still have to do a cartwheel."

"You'll get to Paris."

"I'm planning on it. As of the date of the accident I've made it farther than I did the first time." Closing her eyes, she leaned her head against the back of the couch.

David shifted to hold her in his arms. She quickly moved into his embrace and remained there. He shut his eyes—transported back in time to when they had done this constantly.

Chapter 24

Jillian and Barb were sitting on the rocking chairs on the front porch later that evening. Both had a small glass of wine in their hands. They were laughing about something but stopped when they saw David get out of his car.

"Good, I'm glad you're here," Barb said. "Tell her she shouldn't be overdoing it."

Jillian rolled her green eyes and looked away.

"What did she do?" he asked, worried. He couldn't have anything happen to her now that she was back in his life.

Jillian stuck her chin out. "Hello. I'm right here."

"I came over this afternoon to check on her. She was cleaning the dead flowers out of her pots. I told her she shouldn't be lifting anything, and there she was schlepping around a lawn bag."

Disbelieving, David shook his head. "Jillian, you can't be doing that. You had surgery just last week."

"Omigosh, sorry all. I just hate feeling immobilized. And there were only dead flowers in the bag. It wasn't heavy."

"You still shouldn't be lifting or bending." David looked at the pumpkins and other fall decorations that hadn't been there this morning.

As if reading his thoughts, Barb immediately piped in, "Patrick and I took her out to Levi's nursery. She pointed and we handled. Patrick also cleaned out her beds. I guess we can see where Jillian gets her restlessness from. I swear that man needs a hobby to keep him out of my hair. Do you have any chores at your house that I can send him to do?"

David leaned against the porch rail. "Sorry, I don't. But I'll keep him in mind."

Barb stood and leaned over to kiss Jillian on the cheek. "I'm out of here. Your turn to watch over her now." She patted him on the shoulder. "I made you an apple pie, to say 'thank you.' There's eggplant parmesan in the oven that should be ready in a half hour."

"Thanks, Barb," Jillian said.

David took his place in the vacated rocker—still warm with Barb's body heat. They watched her leave. Shadow came around the corner and stretched out on the top step.

"Jillian, I'm serious. If you need help with something, you ask."

Patting the top of his hand, she said, "You have turned into a big fretter. You know that?"

They sat quietly for a while before David spoke again. "You have a number of pictures of your son, but none of your husband. Why is that?"

"Brian was a good man, but..." She finished the last of her wine. "But I never felt in my heart for him the way I did Danny or..." After a moment, she continued, "With Danny, it was unconditional love. He was my world."

"I'm sorry for your losses," he said.

She remained quiet.

****

Just as Jillian was about to suggest going inside, Luke Walton from the elementary school rode his bicycle up her driveway.

She stood quickly. "Luke, what are you doing here?"

His voice was shaky. "I came by to see if you were okay, Ms. Taylor. Did you get my card?" He walked up the steps.

"I did." She moved toward him. She glanced at David, who was also standing now. She had a bad feeling. It was almost dusk, and Luke was out by himself. "Is everything all right?" she asked.

When he shook his head, Jillian immediately knelt in front of him. "What is it?"

"My dad was in a real bad mood and started throwing things. My mom told me to get out of the house. So I got on my bike and rode. I just decided to come over here."

Jillian rubbed her temples. "Come inside and get something to eat, and we can talk about it before we take you home."

"I can't," he said.

"Can't what?" Jillian asked, gulping.

"Come inside. It wouldn't seem right."

He was right but worry ate at her. It wasn't a good idea for Luke to be out after dark alone. He lived off one of the side streets near the north end of downtown.

Jillian looked over at a puzzled David. "Luke, let us at least take you home."

In the car, she said, "Luke, remember that day in my office when I told you about my friend from school who had a dad like yours? Remember I told you he studied really hard and became a doctor?"

"Yes ma'am."

"Well, this is him." She extended an arm toward David, who was driving. "Dr. Rainer, this is Luke Walton…one of our students at school."

David quickly got the hint. He looked in the rearview mirror, "Hello, Luke. It's very nice to meet you."

"Hello, sir."

Suddenly Luke's face lit up, "Oh, Ms. Taylor, guess what! I met my uncle last weekend, Uncle Rick. He's my mom's brother. We went over to his house. He's married to Aunt Carol, and she says she knows you."

This was too much of a coincidence, "Is their last name McGregor?"

"Yes. They seem nice. My mom and uncle sat for a long time talking. My mom kept apologizing. On the way home, she said if anything happens, I'm to know that I also have them as family."

"That's great Luke." Jillian knew that Carol would move heaven and earth to help people out.

David stopped his Mercedes down the street from where Luke said he lived. Together, he and Luke lifted the bicycle from the trunk. "Thanks for the ride and 'bye Ms. Taylor."

They watched him walk his bike toward his house. They were silent on the quick ride back to Jillian's house where dinner was waiting. "Sad situation that boy has. His father is meaner than a snake, if you know what I mean."

David didn't respond.

Shadow sat by her empty food bowl and meowed.

Jillian opened the oven. Just as she was about to lift

their dinner out, David grabbed the potholders from her.

"Did you not hear what I said earlier?" He took the hot tray out.

"Golly Moses, it's not that heavy," Jillian said defensively.

"Nothing heavier than a gallon of milk." David placed it on a trivet on the counter.

"Thank you." She pulled vegetables from the refrigerator to make a salad.

"So what is Luke's story?" He grabbed plates from the cabinet.

"His family moved here a couple of years ago. Really nice kid, but shows up at school with unexplainable bruises. When I met him, and his family, I thought of you. His father is…I can't even think of the right word."

"A bastard?"

"Yep."

Washing the vegetables, she continued. "My heart goes out to that boy. He has such potential, but his father holds him back. I hate seeing that happen to kids."

Pulling a wine glass and a water glass from her other cabinet, David said, "I know. My thought is he needs someone invested in helping to guide him in making the right choices."

"Like you?" she asked, cutting the vegetables. She wondered how he knew where everything was kept in her cabinets.

"I've made some bad choices," he said quietly.

There was that nine-hundred-pound gorilla sitting in the room that they'd both been avoiding. *Yes, you did,* she thought. She chided herself that it was in the past. *Cathy's long gone and hopefully still in Atlanta.* She knew at some point she and David would need to talk about this. But not tonight.

With the salad made, Jillian scooped a serving of eggplant onto both plates. She pushed the small salad bowls in David's direction for him to fill.

Once they were seated, she said, "You know, you don't need to spend the night." A part of her, though, did want him to stay over. It was comforting knowing he was right there. Another part was disturbed that he *was* right there, but not really with her. Other than yesterday's kiss, when they arrived home, he hadn't made any other overtures. Were the sparks not there for him, like they were for her? *Oh gawd, is he just here out of charity?*

She couldn't let on how hard it was to fall asleep last night knowing he was only across the hall. Her heart sank to her feet and felt as heavy as her cast.

"Someone has to watch over and take care of you," he said, between bites of his dinner.

"And that someone has to be you?" Her voice was light, trying to overcome her inner turmoil.

"Yes." His answer gave no indication of his feelings toward her. In fact, he actually seemed more interested in his food than anything else. He'd always had a healthy appetite, probably left over from his childhood.

Taking a deep breath, Jillian wondered if what she was hoping to rekindle between them no longer existed. He, apparently, was satisfied with being friends.

Watching him devour his food, she asked, "Do you cook for yourself at home?"

Giving her a sideways glance, he said, "Yes, I

know how to cook. I usually pick up something from the market and eat on it for a few days. But I do miss home-cooked meals like this."

So there it was. She was friend-zoned. A friend who provided home-made dinners. *How much better can life get? Ha!*

Chapter 25

As David pulled into Jillian's driveway, he stared at her in utter disbelief. He couldn't believe what she had just said on the drive back from the movies. Since her hospital release, he had spent almost all his free time with her. Did she honestly think he found this to be a burden? The burden was staying at his lonely townhouse after telling her goodnight. Following that second night, she'd insisted he didn't need to keep sleeping in her guest room.

"All I meant was that you don't need to feel obligated to have to drive out here all the time to check on me. Plus, I bought a car today. I'm just waiting to be cleared to drive."

"You bought a car?"

"Yep. Dad, Barb, and I went. They drove it home, since I can't yet. No big deal."

"I would've gone with you."

She opened the door to his car and continued. "David, seriously. I couldn't ask you to do that. You've got work, and they had no problem going with me. I don't want you to think I need babysitting. I have Tara for that."

He slammed the car door harder than he intended. "How many times do I need to tell you, Jillian? I want to do this."

He was not going to say more. He knew from their

younger days she could keep this going, and he'd never win.

Once inside, he walked into the kitchen and poured a glass of water. After all the evenings spent here, he felt like he belonged here. It felt like a home.

He opened the top to the glass container and started to eat the last slice of apple pie.

Jillian stopped untying the scarf around her neck. "You come here for the food, don't you?"

He looked at her sheepishly. "I've been caught." David chuckled when she threw her scarf at him.

She put her elbow on the island, rested her chin in her hand, and smiled. It was the smile that visited him in his dreams. It was the smile that made him feel like he was on top of the world.

"When was the last time you really laughed?" she asked.

"Does it matter?"

"Well it brightens you up. I think you need to laugh more. Even tonight at the movies, you didn't break up that much. It was a comedy, you know."

"I'll try harder."

"You have to do better than that." Jillian took the empty pie plate to the sink to rinse it. She pulled the rubber glove over her one hand with the cast.

He came up behind her to drop off the fork. She turned her head to say "thank you" and went back to rinsing.

Still behind her, David breathed in the scent of her hair. He felt her body stiffen when he pushed her hair to the side and kissed the back of her neck. Goose bumps appeared on her neck as she tilted her head.

Her body was completely still as he continued to

move his mouth along her neck. She finally turned and ran her wet hands up his shirt. He covered her mouth with his. Her breathing was labored, and he heard a small moan escape her lips. He pulled her closer. He had never experienced this sensation with anyone else. *Gawd, I want her so badly.* Just like he had wanted her the first night he slept in the guest room, only a few feet from her.

He pulled back, though he didn't want to let her go. Tara had told him how Jillian's heart had been broken. Yet, since they had been together again, she had not given him any indication he still held the same place in her heart. She'd never said how she really felt.

Her green eyes were staring at him intently.

He let go of her and limped into the sitting room. Lighting the gas logs in her fireplace, he heard her hasty steps following. Shadow rubbed her body against his leg.

"Can I ask you something? How much does it hurt?"

"What?" he asked, turning to her.

"Your hip. I noticed you limping more tonight."

"I missed my swim this morning. And then I was standing in surgery most of the day. This damp, cold weather doesn't help." He joined her on the couch. "Now that it's getting colder, I have to keep working it. Otherwise, it gets stiff, and my limp is more pronounced."

"Are you missing swimming because you're spending so much time…?"

"Jillian, stop it. I want to be here with you, okay? Stop thinking, and saying, it's a burden for me."

He looked at her confused face. "Don't you

understand I want to be here? If that isn't what you want, let me know, and I'll leave."

A grin swept across her face. "I'd like for you to stay."

"Good." He leaned to kiss her forehead.

****

The next morning Tara let herself into Jillian's house. It was becoming a pattern. Jillian started her day with Tara. Around mid-day, either Barb or her dad would come over. Then David would come and spend the evening with her.

"Hey." Tara walked to the coffee pot to pour herself a cupful. "It's going to be a busy day. I have a load of Christmas ornaments arriving today. Did you want to come by and help with the inventory? All you'll be doing is holding a clip board."

"I would love that. I'm going stir-crazy." Jillian finished her coffee. "There's coffee cake in the container. I think I've gained ten pounds since I've been home with all this food Barb keeps making. At least David's been helping to eat it."

Tara gave her the once over, "No, you haven't gained any weight. Barb says you two have been walking around the block a few times each day."

"Yes. And no, I'm not overdoing it." Jillian headed upstairs to change from her yoga pants into something more appropriate to wear to Tara's shop.

Once they were in Tara's SUV with the remainder of the cake in the back seat, Tara asked, "So how's it going with David? Have you two done it yet?"

"No! I can't believe you asked me that. Really?"

"Just wondering. I pretty much expected you two to start up right where you left off."

"I'm not sure where we're at, relationship-wise. He's only kissed me twice. And then he pulls away."

"Did you kiss him back?"

"Of course."

"No. I mean *really* kiss him back." Tara quickly glanced at her before turning her eyes back to the road. "Did you kiss him as though you want him to get naked with you?"

"Yes, I did," Jillian replied defiantly.

They pulled into a parking space behind Tara's Treasures. The fine collectibles shop had been opened soon after her marriage. Over the years the store had grown. Just recently, she moved into this larger space so she could dedicate one section to local artists' works.

Before getting out of the car, Jillian asked, "Do you think, when he had his accident, that certain body parts got damaged?"

Tara cocked her head to the side, "Hmmm, I hadn't thought of that."

"So I could be right in thinking his lack of feelings toward me is because he's been snipped? Maybe he's embarrassed."

"OMG, really? You make it sound like he's a neutered dog." Tara punched in the security code to disarm the alarm.

Setting the coffee cake on the small kitchenette area's table in the back, Jillian shook off her jacket. As she hung it on the coat rack, glancing at the clock, Jillian knew in less than a half hour the three women who worked for Tara would be arriving.

Tara walked through the door into the main part of the store to turn on lights. She returned to the break area.

"I'm only going to say this once…" Jillian confessed, "I think you might be right. I probably didn't put my whole heart into it when David kissed me. Both times I was surprised and wasn't sure what to do."

Dramatically, Tara put her fingers to her chest and acted surprised. "Douth my ears deceive me? Did I hear you say I was right?"

"Yes. You don't need to be so melodramatic."

Tara commented more seriously, "Here's my advice. You make the first move next time and see what happens. Maybe that's what he's waiting for. Subject change. When do you start back at school?"

"Well, I go see most of my doctors tomorrow. David had someone named Helen, from his office, schedule the appointments so I could get them done in one day. If they clear me, I'm hoping to go back on Monday."

"Are you ready?"

"Yes, aside from feeling confined, working might help me think about something other than the fact David's back in my life."

"Is he coming by tonight?"

"No, he has some function at the hospital." Jillian looked over the inventory list. "Seriously? You ordered a case of toffee-covered peanuts?"

"People love them. And you would too if you gave them a try."

"No thanks, I'll stick to ice cream," Jillian said.

"Have you talked to David at all about the break-up? Have you told him how you felt? Have you…?"

Jillian held up her hand and said, "Are you going to let me answer, or are you just going to keep shooting questions at me? I'm not sure why I would need to talk with him about it. Sounds like you already told him everything."

"You are *so* ungrateful. I don't know why I keep you as a friend."

Jillian laughed. "Because I'm the only one who will have you."

Tara replied, "No, I think it's the other way around."

Tara pulled out her razor cutter to open the first box. "You need to talk to him about what happened in Knoxville." She pointed her finger directly at Jillian. "Don't look at me that way. The two of you need to talk, not just listen to a third party's interpretations—even if that third party is me."

"I dunno. I'm scared to bring it up. I'm worried old wounds will be opened."

"Festering wounds need to be opened and drained. Then the real healing can begin." Tara sliced open another box to compare the contents with the packing slip.

"Thank you for those disgusting visuals of wisdom, and for being so honest." Jillian took the sheet of paper from Tara. "I know I'm partly to blame for what happened. I should have talked with him at the time."

"Tell him that," Tara advised. "He needs to hear it from you. Not me."

Jillian whipped around. "Why *do you* feel the need to share everything?"

Opening another box, Tara said, "Here, make sure everything is inside. These people are notorious for missing something."

Moving to another box, she continued, "I might do some of my over-sharing because you bottle everything up inside of you. You're scared to let it out. You loved him once and carried around those memories for years. My only concern would be if you were in love with the memory, and not the man. Now, that you've seen him and what he has become, do you still feel the same?"

Tara was dead-on, but Jillian didn't want to tell her that she was right…again. That would be twice in one day. Instead, she nodded her head; scared to admit aloud that she loved David more than ever.

"I knew I was right," Tara said. "I love being right. And now that you've come to my conclusions, I'll leave you to your checking-off duties. I'll send Suzie back to help when she gets here. And if you're up to it, maybe you can get started on some of the trees."

"No, I won't go that far. No way. I'm not decorating a Christmas tree before Halloween."

"Fine. It was worth a shot," Tara said and laughed. "I guess I better not push you too much today."

Chapter 26

Jillian hated MRIs. Though she'd been ordered to lay still and relax by the technician, relaxation was out of the question with the machine making so much noise. Moving was not possible considering the cramped space, so why even suggest stillness? The indignity of being unhealthy.

Closing her eyes, she recounted yesterday's conversation with Tara. She did need to let David know how she felt—even if he didn't feel the same way.

Then there was the whole matter with their break-up. If she put it all out there, maybe she could have closure. And if David wanted nothing more than friendship, then she would just pull up her big girl panties and accept it. At this point, friendship was better than nothing.

Two hours later, with the MRI complete, the neurologist having cleared her to drive, and her wrist still in a hard cast, she walked to David's office.

Before entering the impressive campus building, she engaged in a little people-watching. It was a perfectly beautiful October day. On a scale of one to ten, she'd give it an eleven. Nothing could ruin this day. Maybe she'd suggest a retrospective walk on the campus tonight before David drove her home.

She went slowly up the four flights of stairs. Opening the door of his well-decorated waiting room, she walked up to the older woman sitting rigidly at the counter. Here was someone who was obviously having a bad day.

Jillian said, "Excuse me, I am here to see David Rainer."

The woman narrowed her eyes, "You'll need to sign in." She pointed to the electronic pad.

"I'm not a patient. I'm, uh, supposed to meet with him today."

The woman sighed loudly. "You'll need to get on the schedule. He's very booked and can't just take walk-ins."

"I'm Jillian Taylor. Can you maybe get Helen? She's the one who made my appointments, and she may—"

The woman's face lit up with recognition. "I'm Helen. It's so nice to meet you, Ms. Taylor. I am sorry. If you had said your name at the beginning…"

Jillian smiled back at her and saw the other woman relax her shoulders. "Helen, thanks so much for making those appointments for me,"

"It was not a problem. David's such a good guy and doesn't ask for much. When he mentioned your needing to try and get all your appointments in one day, I was on it. How are you feeling, by the way?"

"Ready to move on and get back to my normal activities."

Helen leaned forward. "Take all the pampering you can get. That's my motto."

"Thanks, but I'm bored with taking it easy."

"Honey, right now, I would take bored." She paused for a second. "If you don't mind me saying—and I'm not saying he was a grump before—Dr. Rainer sure has been happier these last few weeks."

Jillian's stomach did happy flips. Her smile broadened. "Really?" she asked, feeling like a school girl. Maybe, just maybe, he still had feelings for her.

Helen's features hardened. "Yeah. This ball of fire coming in the door now could use a big dose of happy. Can't stand the woman."

Jillian turned to see her nemesis. Her heart and stomach dropped to the ground floor. Her body went rigid. *What the hell is she doing here?*

Not even acknowledging her, Cathy walked right up to the desk. "Is David in?" she demanded. "I've left him several messages today."

Helen gave Cathy a blank stare.

Jillian was fearful a catfight was about to break out.

"He's with a patient and has two more to see."

"Well, I can't tell you how important it is I talk with him," Cathy sniped condescendingly. "Please make sure he knows I'm here waiting for him."

When Helen didn't move, Cathy flipped her hand. "I need to see him. Now!"

"I'll give him the message, *after* he's done with his patients."

Cathy shook her head in disgust. Her eyes finally landed on Jillian.

Jillian, still in shock, couldn't believe she was right here. When they were younger, Cathy's nastiness detracted from her beauty. It had gotten worse over the years.

At that moment, Jillian decided she would not cower. In fact she stood a bit taller, what with Helen taking all this in.

Startled, Cathy said, "I know you. You're uh—"

"Jillian O'Malley Taylor," she said sweetly, knowing full well Cathy knew who she was. "And how are you, Cathy?"

"What a surprise to see you here," she said haughtily. "David hasn't mentioned you—not even last night at the sponsorship dinner."

Still smiling, Jillian didn't respond. She knew her words would get twisted. Also, as she was just as surprised to see Cathy, she didn't want to risk having her voice shake. *Why is this she-devil constantly showing up?*

"Are you here to see David?" Cathy barked.

"Yes, she is." Helen's wink to Jillian made it obvious whose side she was on.

Cathy gave Jillian a once-over and glanced back to Helen. "Please tell him I was here, and it is imperative we talk. Can you remember that?"

Helen bit back. "I think I can."

Together they watched Cathy storm from the office.

"Not sure what the story is there. Dr. Rainer seems to be her only friend here, using that term loosely. That one's been very busy making enemies."

With Cathy's exit, Jillian felt suddenly tired. She just wanted to go home now. The day had gone right from an eleven to a one. Peter didn't work that far away. Maybe she'd call him to come by and pick her up.

Jillian looked at the filled waiting room before turning back to Helen. "You know what? I think I'm going to head out. He still has a few more patients, and I could use a nap. Tell him I was here."

"Are you sure, Jillian?"

"Yes. And it was nice meeting you, Helen. Thanks again for helping out with the scheduling for me."

"Not a problem, dear."

Jillian walked out of the office to call Peter.

"Sure. I'll meet you out front in about fifteen minutes."

Waiting outside, she saw Eric jogging by.

He stopped when he recognized her. "I'd give you a hug, but I am all sweaty." He walked in small circles with his hands on top of his head.

"That's fine, I'll take a pass," she said.

"What are you doing here?" He looked up at the building in front of them.

"I had a bunch of appointments, and then David was going to take me home. But he has some more patients. So, Peter, Tara's husband, is going to pick me up."

"Jillian, I can tell from your voice something's wrong. What happened?"

"Cathy came into his office," she blurted out. "She was with him last night. What the hell is she doing here?"

The look on Eric's face confirmed her suspicions. They stood in silence looking at each other. Finally, Eric said, "He hates her, you know."

"That doesn't seem to matter to her." She looked down at her fingernails.

"Don't let this get between you two. He's changed now that you're back in his life. He seems more alive than he has in years."

Jillian was about to reply when Peter pulled up to a stop in front of her. "I'll see you later, Eric." Jillian gave him a peck on his cheek.

On the way home, she didn't mention the run-in with Cathy to Peter. Tara would have a fit if he knew before she did. Instead they talked about the twins getting their licenses.

****

Having seen his last patient of the day, David was standing in the hall outside one of the exam rooms getting his schedule for the next day. Dan, one of his medical schoolmates, and another cardiologist in the group casually mentioned he'd heard from one of his patients about an uncomfortable confrontation between two women in the waiting room.

The hair on the back of David's neck immediately stood up when, at the same time, Helen came up to him. From the pinched look on her face, he knew the identities of the two women. He trailed Helen into his office and got a firsthand account of the events. Dan, who had followed, also stood listening and, being acquainted with both women, offered his own commentary.

He hated that, once again, Jillian had run when Cathy was around. David needed to put an end to this, once and for all. First, David should do damage-control with Jillian, to be followed by a conversation with Cathy that would leave no room for misinterpretation.

After picking up two dozen roses at the florist's, David sped to Jillian's house. He didn't feel comfortable just walking in so waited for her to answer the doorbell. When the door finally opened, she looked weary.

He shifted the large arrangement of roses. "May I come in?"

"I guess," she responded tentatively.

Setting the roses on the kitchen island, he said, "These are for you."

"Are you feeling guilty about something?" One eyebrow rose.

"No. I heard you had a rough day. I want us to talk. I want to be sure you to know how I feel."

She crossed her arms, "About Cathy?"

"About everything. First, how did your doctors' visits go today?"

"Fine. I go back to work on Monday, which will be nice. The school will be all abuzz with Halloween by next Friday."

He observed her closely. "Don't overdo it."

She took a single wine glass out of the cabinet.

Walking up to her, he removed the glass from her hand set it on the counter, and took her hands in his. "Jillian, I'm so sorry about what happened in Knoxville. I've played it over in my mind a million times. Looking back, I don't blame you for what you did. I just wish we could've talked and worked it out afterward."

Her shoulders sagged. "You broke my heart, David." She looked at him, directly. Her green eyes were glistened with tears that wanted to come. "I know Eric and Tara filled you in about my history since then—the two big mouths. But I want to hear from you. What happened?" Her face was sad, almost defeated. Her hands felt tense.

"I was so intent on providing for us and not bringing all my student bills into the marriage, that I never realized how much I was working, and how that was negatively affecting you. Or rather, us. I kept thinking we had all the time in the world in front of us."

Shaking her head, Jillian pulled her hand from his. "Not realize? How can you say that?"

He followed her into the sunroom, where she closed the windows. He sat on the couch. It felt as if he'd been punched in the stomach when she took a seat in the chair. He got up and moved the footstool to sit in front of her, their knees touching.

"Stupidity, on my part. I never looked at it from your viewpoint. I was too focused on me."

He rested his hand on her knees. "Anyways, when the head of cardiology at the hospital in Knoxville hosted a cocktail party and I received an invitation, I jumped at the chance. Cathy happened to call the same day I received the invite. Stupid me told her about it. She'd been having a hard time adjusting in Atlanta. She jumped at the chance to go, to make some professional connections."

Jillian pushed his hands from her knees and rested her own clenched hands in her lap.

"I told her I was going to call you, but she pointed out the opportunity for networking that might make it possible for her to get a transfer. I agreed, even though I really wanted you there. In fact, the day before I called and left a message for her not to come. I missed you and wanted to see you."

David ran his hands through his hair before he looked her straight in the eyes. "I knew you and the others were to go to Keeneland, but I hoped I might change your mind. My mistake was waiting to confirm that she got my message before I called you. I was sure it would be awkward to have you both there."

She cocked her head to the side. "See how well that

worked out?"

"I know." He picked her hand up in his. "When you walked in, I was stunned. The minute I saw you, I knew what would happen when you saw her. The look of pain and betrayal on your face said it all."

Jillian focused on her rigid hand before meeting his eyes. "You looked so handsome that night. I don't think I'd ever seen you in a suit. And she...she looked so glamorous. I felt stupid and out of place standing there." She looked back at him. "You just stood there and didn't say anything."

"I didn't know what to say. After you left, I thought of plenty to say. I let Cathy know she'd destroyed the one thing more important to me than life itself."

She tore her eyes from his but not before he saw a tear fall from her cheek. She pulled her hand from his to wipe it away.

As painful as talking about this was, he needed to tell her that he was going to stop at nothing to have her back in his life. He leaned forward to prop his knees on his elbows, exhaling all the stress built up inside him. "You said you never wanted to see me again. I tried calling. I even reached out to Eric who, by the way, took your side one hundred percent."

Silence and tension hung in the room. The only sound came from the wind chimes moving in the breeze outside the door.

"A few months later, I drove up again. I had to see you, and I wanted to explain." He stopped to stare into her face. "I missed you so much, Jillian. Granted we had gone long periods without seeing each other, but I always knew you were there. This time it was different.

When Eric told me you had moved, but he didn't know where, I felt like I had died. There was nothing inside of me. I had no place to go."

He pushed himself from the stool and limped slowly to the window. On the table there was a picture of Tara, Peter, and Jillian in front of Greece's Parthenon. He picked it up.

"I never returned your ring to the store. In the beginning, I kept it. Hoping. After a while it was a reminder of how my ambitions and stupidity caused you so much pain. I'd lie in bed at night holding it. I hated myself. The only thing I had left was work, so I worked non-stop...and shut myself off from everyone else."

He turned to look at her sitting on the chair. Her face was still.

"When I saw you that day in the ER, I was so scared. And then I heard your last name. I'll say it. I was hurt and angry. Even that first night I came here, I was mad. You got married and had a family."

"You were mad at me?" she asked in shock.

"Yes, because I was supposed to be your husband. I was supposed to be the one with you when you had cancer. I would have taken care of you. And I was mad at *me* because I had been weak and couldn't stand up to her. So instead you had someone else help you through."

Jillian quickly went into the kitchen to grab tissues. She hovered in the doorway. "What happens to us now?" she asked, quietly crossing her arms. "I don't know what you want."

"I want you back in my life, but I'm afraid you don't want the same. When I kissed you, I felt you holding back. When I hold you in my arms, I don't want to let you go. But I don't know if you trust me"—he walked to stand in front of her—"especially considering how you took off when you ran into Cathy at the office today."

Her arms dropped to her side. "I think things happen for a reason. Maybe back then was the wrong time for us. As much as it hurt, maybe we were destined to be apart...so we'd be better able to appreciate what we have. I always wondered what became of you but was too scared to find out."

"I thought about you all the time, Jillian. I couldn't fall in love because of you," he said.

Her green eyes blinked, and he knew he had said something wrong. They stood staring, the only movement being the tear that trailed down her cheek.

"You need to get some rest," he said gruffly. He walked past her into the kitchen. "I need to go. I won't hurt you again."

He picked up his keys from the counter and looked at her one last time

****

Jillian was frozen to the floor, shivering, unsure if the reason was the cool outdoor air coming inside or the words he'd said.

"No," she yelled, spinning around. "You are not leaving."

She surprised herself and him.

"I never loved Brian the way I loved you. It was unfair to him. And when I went through chemo, both times, it was you that I wanted. Once I remember thinking, 'I have to get better just to be able to see David *one* more time.'"

With a sudden nervous energy, she pulled her hair off her face into a ponytail. "After Danny and Brian died, I heard Tara whispering to Barb about trying to find you, so maybe you could help me. But I was a mess, and I didn't want you to see me like that." She rolled her eyes.

"I'd have been there," he said. "I'd drop everything to be with you. That's why I got so upset the other day when you told me I didn't have to help you. You didn't want me as a taxi-driver." He walked up to stand in front of her. "I want to be here now, Jillian…for you."

"Okay," she said. "But I have two requests."

"What?" he asked.

"Cathy is no more."

"Agreed!"

She closed the space between then and ran her fingers over his lips. "And I want you to smile more."

She kissed him passionately, pouring her entire being into it. She ran her hands through his hair. Her entire body, on fire, was pressed against his. Touching him made a tingle she hadn't felt in years run up her spine.

Their tongues twined together and his erection pressed against her. "And one other thing…" She unbuttoned his shirt. "Make love to me."

With his shirt and t-shirt lying on the floor, she caressed his firm chest. She felt his skin tighten beneath her touch. She loved the feel of him. She lightly ran her fingertips up and around his neck to pull him toward her.

His mouth claimed hers as if he would never release her again. His tongue thrust into her mouth and delicately touched hers. She felt, as well as heard, the moan in his throat. Her body arched into his and there was an immediate response. She pulled him tighter to her and continued to make love to his mouth.

For the first time that night, she saw warmth return to his eyes. She took his hand to lead him upstairs. She didn't want their first re-uniting to be on the cold kitchen counter.

With his help, she pulled the sweater over her head, feeling self-conscious of how her breasts without any nipples looked in the lace bra. He would know as soon as he touched them, they were not real.

"I've missed you more than you'll ever know, Jillian." He opened his arms to embrace her.

She continued the assault on his mouth. He pulled her body closer. His hands ran over her back and held her tight.

His stiffness pressed against her again. She ran her fingers down his stomach, pulled at the button on his pants, and pushed them down. Once she had him naked, she pulled him toward the bed as she wiggled out of her pants.

A fire blazed in her eyes when she pushed him down onto the bed and climbed on top of him. She kissed his mouth, neck, and chest. For the first time in twenty years, her body felt alive with excitement and anticipation.

She looked down at him. His eyes watched with intense desire. Her eyes never left his. She let her hands run over his hips, pausing ever so slightly on the injured one. She kissed the scars on his left hip.

With uncontrolled passion, she moved her lips to his face. She rubbed her female parts over him, teasing before he entered her. Her insides squeezed him.

He rotated his hips as they tenderly made love to each other. When they climaxed together, she moaned his name and held him tight.

Lying in his arms, she was tired, yet more alive than she had been in years. "I love you," she whispered.

He kissed her and echoed her words. They lay together, naked, her head resting in the crux of his arm. She threw her leg over his and ran her fingers through his chest hairs.

He let go of her briefly to turn the light off.

With the room engulfed in darkness, she whispered, "I always liked sleeping with you like this. Feeling you. You would never let go of me. I've missed that."

"I missed you more," he whispered back.

"Then stay the night with me." She lightly caressed his arm.

"Gladly," he said, with a smile in his voice.

His hand ran alongside her breasts, "They're bigger than I remember."

"Meet my fake size Bs," she said. She loved the feel of his hands on her.

"Nice to meet you," he said into her ear and gave them a little pinch. He continued to play with her breasts, arousing her.

She arched her back, signaling she was ready for more. His hand travelled teasingly down her body. Rolling onto her back, she locked her lips onto his. He was on top now driving into her.

This time it was more urgent, releasing the many years of pent-up frustration she had been unaware of. She missed the weight of his body, the feel of him inside her, and his gentle caresses. Finally, she was relaxed enough to fall asleep next to the person Nana had said was her soul mate. The one who made her tingle all over.

Chapter 27

It was still dark when David opened his eyes. They adjusted, and he looked about the room. Jillian's naked body was pressed against him, and it wasn't a dream this time. Her cast rested on his stomach.

The clock next to the bed read five o'clock. As much as he didn't want to leave her side, he had to get up to head to the pool and then to the hospital. With it being Friday, he typically only worked until noon. Maybe they could go to Keeneland and watch the horse races with some of the other doctors in the group.

Moving slowly from the bed, so as not to wake her, he gathered up his clothes. Making his way down the stairs, without tripping over Shadow, he left her a note on the counter about his idea for the afternoon.

After sleeping with Jillian and swimming, he felt doubly invigorated. Pulling into his assigned parking space in the garage, the mood was spoiled. There stood Cathy, waiting for him. Her arms were crossed and she looked completely pissed.

He took a deep breath to brace himself for what was coming next. He stepped from his car. "What do you want?" he asked.

"Really, David. Is that how you talk to your friends?" Her pretense at being hurt was unimpressive. "Did you forget? I came up here to be with you."

"Well, then, you came here for absolutely the

wrong reason. I didn't ask you to come." Opening the car's back door, he pulled out his bag

"I saw Jillian at your office yesterday. Breast cancer twice, huh? Not good odds if you think about it for the long-haul."

His blood pressure rose. "And just how did you find that out?"

"I have my ways." She tilted her head to the side, acting coy. "I can't believe you'd want to reconnect—"

"Cathy, you need to shut up!"

"Oh, are you saying that if I played the part of a victim, I could get your attention again?"

"You never had my attention. You were a fellow student, and that was it. I never had any feelings for you. In fact, the only thing I feel for you now is contempt."

"Really? Is that so? So what was it we had in Atlanta? Or when I first came up here?"

"It was you inserting yourself into my life. And I am saying, beginning right now, no more! Stay out of my life, Cathy."

"David, I just want us to be friends," she pleaded. "Will you please give me a second chance? Can you give that to me?"

"Second chance? There've been a lot more than that. You don't know how to be a friend. I don't trust you. You ruined something for me twenty years ago, and I know your intentions are to try it again. I can't forgive you." He stormed off to the elevator.

She licked her lips walking quickly to keep up with him. For once he wasn't the slow one. "Listen, I'm sorry about what happened. Seriously, that was a long time ago, and it seems as though you keep forgetting, *she* left *you*! Doesn't that tell you something?"

The elevator came. "Cathy! Why don't you just shut up?"

"No," she shouted. The sound reverberated against the walls of the steel enclosure. Lowering her voice, she continued. "I'm not ready to give up on us, David."

David abruptly turned toward her, "Listen to me. There never was, and there will never be an *us*. Jillian's back in my life, and I couldn't be happier. The only thing that could possibly make me happier is for you to leave the city." He pointed a finger at her. "And stay away from Jillian. You got that? I am not letting you come between us anymore."

When the elevator opened on his office floor, he limped off alone. He didn't look back when he heard her sniffle.

****

The sound of the horse hooves hitting the ground was louder than she remembered. It had been years since Jillian and Tara had gone to Keeneland in the fall. They usually went in the spring, all decked out in sundresses and hats. This time, they had on boots, black pants, and long sleeves. Tara had on a fringed poncho.

When Jillian had come down the stairs that morning, Tara was already on the phone in her kitchen with a cup of coffee. She pointed at the note while explaining to Peter he was taking the rest of the day off to head to the races.

With her conversation with Peter over, Tara asked, "Something to tell me?"

"Going to Keeneland with us today, are you?"

"Yes. I figure if he left you a note that means he spent the night. My question is what room did he sleep in?"

Jillian smiled inwardly at the note. "Mine." She poured herself a cup of coffee. Over coffee and quiche, she shared everything that happened yesterday, starting with the doctor visits, including seeing Cathy, David's confession, and ending with them in bed. She gave the G-rated version.

After hearing Tara's take on everything, with the word "bitch" used multiple times, Jillian felt better. Remembering that in a little over a month, she would hit her five-year mark of being cancer-free put her mood over the top.

Now they were sitting in the box seats watching the horses run by at full speed. There were two other physicians from David's group in the box. One raised his bushy eyebrows when David had introduced her, along with Tara and Peter, to everyone. Dan, whom they remembered from school, was happy to see the two women.

Dan's wife, Rachel, was petite. Tara and Jillian towered over her little frame. Suggesting they sit, she promptly said, "You look very familiar. I know I've seen you before."

"I own Tara's Treasures over in Vickery," Tara volunteered. Typically, she figured everyone shopped at her store and life centered around her.

"I love that store," Rachel exclaimed, clapping her hands together. "I bet that's it. I loved what you did with the Halloween decorations. I can't tell you how many of your ghosts I bought this year. They are all around the house."

Looking over her shoulder and then turning back, she lowered her voice. "When are you putting out the

Christmas decorations? I usually go several times and sneak the stuff in without Dan knowing."

Jillian shook her head. "No, Christmas doesn't go up until after Halloween."

Tara pointed her thumb to Jillian. "See what I have to deal with. I asked her the other day if I could start decorating just one tree with the newly-arrived ornaments, and she threw a fit."

"Dan told me you're a school principal?" Rachel said.

"Yes, that's me." Jillian noticed David watching her.

"I know I'm being nosy, a bad habit of mine, unlike Maura here who's so quiet. But I have to know, what's the story with you and David?" Rachel asked. "I mean in the entire time I have known him, which is from the day he moved here, he's never mentioned a girlfriend or anyone. So when Dan told me this morning that David was bringing someone he had been engaged to after college, I was floored."

Jillian had to think for a minute. She didn't want to delve too deeply. When Tara nudged her arm, she said, "Yes, we were once together, but the timing wasn't right. A freak accident brought us back together."

"Aww, how romantic," Rachel said.

Tara and Jillian shared a look. If she only knew.

David came over. "Do you need anything?"

Tara pointed at him. "We need to talk. Later."

Jillian saw David's grin but couldn't venture to guess what little secret the two were hatching. "I'd like a glass of wine," she said.

"Me, too," said Tara, batting her eyelashes. "And tell Peter he better pick a good horse." She stood. "Oh never mind, I'll have to help him."

When they were out of earshot, Rachel leaned in. "You two make a really handsome couple with your dark hair and your height. In fact, when you walked in, Dan and I both commented on it."

"Thank you." Jillian felt the warmth that comes from being referred to as a couple.

David returned and handed her the glass of wine. He set his beer on the table and took the seat Tara had vacated. He opened the program and asked Jillian if there were any horses in the next races she wanted to bet on.

Together they reviewed the names and stats. Well, he reviewed the stats, and she looked at the names. Once they made their picks, he left to go place their bets but not before leaning over to kiss her.

"Oh gawd. Get a room, will ya?" Tara said with a smirk. "Wait, David. I'm placing our bets. Peter can't be trusted to do it properly."

When David laughed, there was a quick moment of silence from the group. Jillian wondered if they noticed the same thing. He finally seemed relaxed and at ease.

Peter winked at her. "In all the time I've known you, Jillian, I've never seen you look like this."

"Like what?" she asked innocently.

"Okay, let me put it this way." He dropped his voice. "You never looked at Brian the way you look at David."

She beamed. Peter was right. She hadn't felt this way in a long time.

Chapter 28

Jillian made it through the first week of school with no problems. She was, of course, exhausted by the end of each day. The worst was getting into her new car that first morning. Her hands shook, remembering the last time she'd been behind a wheel.

Thankfully David wasn't there to witness her small panic attack. He'd have driven her to school, like a child. She needed to show herself, and everyone else, she was okay.

The kids at the school greeted her eagerly. Her office was festooned with the cards and posters each of the classes had made. It took her two days, but she visited each classroom to say thank you. She even sat with a few tables of children at lunch.

Friday—she was glad for the weekend, especially with the kids overexcited for Halloween tomorrow. The entire school seemed to be a pre-sugar high of activity.

She had just finished getting ready when David arrived. He knocked on the side door, as usual, before walking in. Her garage was connected to the house with the covered passage that Brian had built in anticipation of the move that didn't become a fact.

"Okay, you've spent every night here for the last week. I don't think you need to knock anymore."

"Just trying to be polite," he said.

Opening a kitchen drawer, Jillian pulled out a key.

She put it in his hand. "Here. No more knocking."

He leaned in and kissed her, and she eagerly accepted. Pressing her against the counter, he continued his assault on his mouth until her lips were swollen. Her fingers ran up his chest and started to undo his shirt.

He unzipped her black dress, and it fell off her shoulders. He kissed her neck and trailed down to her breasts. Soon her bra and the rest of her clothes lay in a pile on the floor. She stripped his clothing just as efficiently and they made love in the kitchen. With her legs wrapped around him, she moaned his name and bit his chest.

When they were done, she leaned against him, loving his musky smell. "Hmm, I wonder what would happen, if I gave you a small space to put your clothes?"

Kissing her nose, he said, "Do it and find out."

"That will have to wait for tomorrow. Speaking of which…" She kissed him back. "I've never seen your place. Since we'll be in Lexington, won't it be easier to stay there? Or is there something you're hiding?"

"We can stay there if you want. It's not all comfy like this place. But what about Shadow?" His hands slid along her bare back.

"We'll give her some food and leave a light on. She'll be fine. I'd like to see where you live."

"Then go pack your bag, and we'll spend the night there."

"Ahh, an adventure." She picked her clothes up off the floor and went upstairs to freshen up as she was certain she smelled of sex.

With the cat fed, and her overnight bag in the backseat, they drove back into Lexington to have dinner at Portofino's.

They dropped the car with the valet and held hands walking into the restaurant. Eric and Lynda were already at the table when they arrived.

"Sorry we're late." Jillian sat in the chair David held for her.

"Not to worry," Lynda said.

"It feels like old times, seeing you together like this," Eric said.

Jillian licked her lips and looked to David.

With a hearty laugh, Eric added, "Just don't get all lovey-dovey on me while I'm trying to eat, okay?"

Changing the subject, Lynda asked, "How are you feeling, Jillian?"

"Tired, but it's good to be back at work and being productive. Plus, I was getting tired of being driven around."

"What? Don't you like my driving?" David looked at the waiter asking for their drink orders.

When David studied the wine menu and ordered a Pinot Noir for the table, Jillian was a bit stunned.

Eric said, "I let David order the wines when we're out. I always picked the cheapest one on the menu."

Lynda rolled her eyes.

"Are you going to swirl it around when it comes to the table?" Jillian asked.

"Yes, to make sure it has good legs."

"When did you become a wine snob?" she asked.

"When I was in Atlanta. I went to a wine club to learn," he said dryly. "It became a hobby."

"Uh-oh, what is your take on the wine I have at the house."

"It's a good casual wine."

"Okay, haven't heard that before, but I'll take it," she said, patting his upper arm.

The waiter brought the wine and took their food order. David did test it, as promised. Jillian withheld a laugh remembering his social struggles when they were younger. Now he was a classy, well-bred doctor.

Over dinner, they shared stories of their younger days at school with Lynda and laughed at some of the fun they had. There was no awkwardness when the conversation turned to the times when Jillian wasn't a part of their lives. She loved the stories, hearing a little more of David's history.

David would touch her knee as though reassuring her he was there. Thankfully, there was no talk of cancer, her accident, and especially not their breakup.

As they consumed their after-dinner drinks, Jillian thought she might explode with all the food she had eaten. When the waiter asked about dessert, she found herself sharing cheesecake with David.

When it was time to leave, David stood to help her with her chair. That's when she saw Cathy—sitting at a table, by herself, facing them. Jillian looked at David.

Taking her hand in his, he brought it to his lips and leaned in close to whisper in her ear. "You are mine," he said. "You are the only one I've ever wanted to be with."

She smiled at him. With his hand on her lower back, they exited the restaurant.

Looking back at the window, she saw Cathy had a clear line of sight at David's arm around her waist. Maybe it was the alcohol, or maybe she was a female marking her territory, but Jillian leaned in to kiss David and gave him plenty of tongue action while she was at it.

"What did I say about being all kissy-face?" Eric asked.

"Hey, can't help it," Jillian said. "Making up for lost time.

****

David knew immediately what Jillian was doing while they waited for the valet. He had seen Cathy come into the restaurant and watch them all evening. He hadn't said anything to save the night from ruin.

He sensed her eyes watching while they waited for the car. Jillian's kisses made other body parts stand up and take notice. It was rather sexy how she had no problems staking her claim on him.

He drove the short ride to his townhouse. He waited for the gate to open before pulling into the community.

"Fancy," she said, with a low whistle.

"I like it. It has a view of the lake." David pulled into the garage on the front of his unit.

She looked around at the empty garage that contained only his car and his garbage can. "Wow, you're one of the few people I know who use your garage only for its intended purpose."

He grabbed her bag from the back seat, opened the door adjoining the kitchen, and turned on the lights.

She walked to the back window that overlooked the lake. "Beautiful view."

He went up behind her to wrap his arms around her waist. "You certainly are," he whispered in her ear. Pushing her hair aside, he kissed her neck, running his hands across her breasts.

"You...know...what I...meant," she said, in short

breaths.

She turned to pull his face to hers but nearly punched him in the eye with her cast. "Sorry about that." She kissed his cheek, his eye, and then covered his face with kisses before breaking away. "First, I want to see the place you call home."

Jillian looked around at the black and gray contemporary decor. No antiques or photographs here. He had acquired a few paintings, but they were modern in design.

She stroked the dining room's glass tabletop and black chairs before circling back into the family room. She walked to the couch to sit, testing it. "Not what I would have expected, but at least there is nothing to make me run in fear. Though I can't exactly see myself flopping on this couch to read a book or watch a movie."

"So you don't like it," he stated matter-of-factly.

"Hey, as long as you're comfortable, that's what's important. I'm just saying, it's not my style."

Picking up the remote, he dimmed the lights to a low level and turned on the fire place. Sitting next to her, he pulled her close. "*You* are my style."

"Really?" Her eyes lit up when he slid his hand up her dress.

He was hard and wanted her, right now. She stood and walked over to close the curtains to the lake while he undid his pants. Standing in front of him, she let her dress drop to the floor and undid her bra. He slid her panties down to the floor stroking every part of her from the waist down before she straddled his lap. She slowly took off his shirt, and they made love on his couch.

It had never been quite like this before as they became one. They continued to make love upstairs in his bedroom, and then in the shower.

When they were sated, they lay on his bed, cuddled together. Her leg draped over his. "I'll give you this...at least the bed is comfortable." She ran her fingers along his chest.

"What didn't you like about the couch?"

"It was rather stiff," she said.

"As was I," he said, grinning.

Her eyes twinkled. "I noticed. And you need some pictures."

"I have some on the wall." He stroked the lower part of her back.

"You know what I mean. Photographs..." Sitting up, she leaned across him, and opened up his nightstand drawer. "I'll bet you have some in here."

"Jillian, what are you doing?" He anxiously tried to pull her back.

"Oh? What's hiding in here that you don't want me to see?" She flipped over him and was sitting on his side of the bed. Turning on the light, she reached in and held the velvet box that contained the engagement ring from long ago.

Jillian opened the box to look at it. She slid the ring onto her finger and held her hand up. "After all these years, it still fits," she said.

Looking at the small ring on her hand—it was all he could afford back then—he was embarrassed. "Let me have it back."

She peered into the drawer he tried to shut and pushed his hand away. There were pictures in the drawer—photos of the two of them together along with a few magazines with her on the cover. When she turned to face him, he looked away.

Putting the shots down, she lifted his hand to her face. "I'm here now, David. And not planning on leaving any time soon."

His eyes met hers. There was no pity, just her love…and the smile. The smile that the camera loved—the one that was only for him. He wasn't going to let her go ever again.

Chapter 29

They had fallen into a comfortable routine in the last weeks. David stayed almost every night at her place, agreeing that it was by far the more relaxed of the two. Maybe she was old-fashioned, but she wasn't ready for him to officially move in with her. Thankfully, he hadn't broached the subject.

There were some of his things in the bathroom and a few sets of clothes in the closet, but that was it. Not once had she seen any of his things in the laundry. That would have been an official sign that they were shacking up.

They were going to meet Peter and Tara for drinks and appetizers at Barney's Pub downtown. She and David decided to walk there.

"When do you go for your MRI and ultrasound?" he asked.

"Thanksgiving week," she said. "I can't wait. Not that I am wishing my life away. I just want to get to the five-year mark and celebrate making it."

"Do you want me to go with you?"

She stopped in the middle of the sidewalk to look at him. He was so serious and concerned. "No, 'cuz you'll just be sitting in the waiting room while they do all their poking and prodding."

His face was still tense as they walked. "I can be there for moral support."

They walked a little farther before she answered, "Okay, but don't get all doctor-like on me."

"I'll try not to," he said, grinning.

She slapped his shoulder. "I mean it, David."

They continued down the pavement. "You know, it's weird, but it was only when the cancer came back, I finally realized how precious life was. Not that I didn't the first time. But it hit me harder…probably because Danny and Brian had passed away. I knew I wanted to live, and beat this, and enjoy every remaining day I was given. I just kept thinking 'I have to hit the five-year mark.' And here it is, so close I can feel it."

He squeezed her hand. "It will be good news, Jillian. I can feel it."

"It will." They stopped at the flashing *Don't Walk* light at the intersection. "Emily asked me the other day if I had been practicing my cartwheels. She says we have to do five in a row this year."

"Have you?"

"Hell no," she said as they crossed the street to the town green. Barney's was on the other side of the square.

"You're close with Emily and Kyle, aren't you?" David asked.

"Tara and Peter stopped short of shared custody, but they are my adopted children. I always wanted kids and well…that's not happening."

"I'm sorry, Jillian. I know you miss Danny." He squeezed her hand.

"Don't be. I can't do anything about it. And as Nana would say, 'can't cry over spilled bourbon.'"

"Isn't is milk?"

"It's Nana we're talking about, don't forget."

"You're right," he said.

Right outside Barney's Pub, David stopped. Jillian tilted her head questioningly.

David said, "Oh…before I forget, I heard head of anesthesia at the medical center is a bit disenchanted with our 'friend.'"

"Interesting." It was hard for Jillian to keep the glee from her voice, but karma did have a way of showing up when you least expected it.

"Yep, too many complaints from the surgeons," he said. "Seems no one can stand working with her."

"Hmm. Has she been bothering you at the office lately?"

"No. Helen intercepts all her messages."

"Way to go, Helen."

They walked into the pub where Peter and Tara had scored a table. David seemed so relaxed. She liked that.

Chapter 30

Looking at the clock, David knew he should give Jillian a call to let her know he would be late. It was already after seven and would probably be another hour before he would be able to leave.

Walking through the enclosed crosswalk back to his office, his stomach growled. The cafeteria in his building was closed, and the least appetizing thing he could think of was eating at the hospital. Lindy's, down the street, would still be open. He could grab a sandwich there.

Making his way down to the first floor, he stepped out into the chilly night air. Not counting that morning, when he got into his car, this was the first time he had been outside all day. Thinking it might be easier to spend the night at his place, he pulled out his phone to call Jillian. Before her phone had a chance to ring, he remembered there was a Parent Booster meeting she was attending. He instead texted,—*Still at work. Call me. May spend night in Lex.*—

Luckily there was no one in line at Lindy's. He walked up to the counter and placed his order for a turkey on rye.

"Well, well, well. He emerges." Cathy was standing next to him.

"What?" he asked, annoyed at the very sound of her voice.

Her steely gaze was on him. "Well, I never see you around anymore. And if I do, then you're with *her*."

His phone buzzed in his pocket. He pulled it out hoping it was Jillian calling. "Excuse me." He walked away from Cathy and moved to the cashier to pay for his sandwich.

"Hey there," he said.

"The meeting just ended and I saw your text," she said. "That's a bummer."

Cathy quickly appeared at his side. "I've got both sandwiches," she said to the cashier. "I'm the grilled chicken, and he's the turkey rye."

"Jillian, hold on a second." David held the phone away. "I've got my own."

"David, it's the least I can do since you're helping me out."

"What the hell are you talking about?" David was futilely trying to keep his temper in check.

Cathy sighed loudly, "Did you forget we had plans?"

He looked at the cashier. "Ring up her sandwich only. I'm paying for mine separately. I'll be right back." He stormed outside.

"Jillian?" He wondered what she had heard.

"Are you with Cathy? And is that the reason you're staying at your place tonight?"

Yep, she'd heard. "I'm at Lindy's getting a sandwich to take back to the office to work. She came in after me."

"So what are you helping her out with?"

"Nothing."

"You said that pretty quickly."

"Jillian," he said taking a deep breath. "I'm not

helping her with anything. If you want to come down and watch me eat and work, you can. I think you'll notice I'll be alone."

"David. I'll wait for you to walk me back." Cathy had appeared at his side.

He glared at Cathy's innocent smile. The woman really did have no limits.

"Jillian, I'm grabbing my sandwich, swinging by the office, and then I'll be home. I'll see you in less than an hour. I love you."

"Love you too. 'Bye." She hung up her phone.

David glared at Cathy.

"What? Is she jealous? That's not a good sign in any relationship," Cathy said.

"Do you have a death wish?" he asked. "And what, in God's name, do you imagine I am helping you with?"

"I bought a place in your complex. I wanted to see if you could be there when the movers come. I don't think it's a good idea being there by myself when they're there. I mean...you *are* only two doors down."

Two doors! Well, why wasn't she right next to him, where she'd probably put in a peep hole?

This only moved up what he needed to do. He stormed back into the deli to pick up, and pay for, his sandwich. Walking back to the office, he didn't acknowledge or talk with Cathy, though she stayed right by his side.

Chapter 31

The Cancer Center was a block from his building. All the time he had worked here, David had never stepped inside the huge building. He knew of the research and the advances they were making, but his job required no need to visit.

The several-stories-high glass made the building bright with natural light. There were pictures of people on every wall, some with bald or scarf-covered heads. He slowed to look at the photos, some of which were poster-sized. One, on the wall above the elevators, was captioned *We Will Win the Fight*.

To the right was a gray stone rectangular block engraved *For Those Who Fought Bravely*. There were more names than was equitable listed. "My goal was to keep my name from being added to that," Jillian said.

Though he dealt on a daily basis with patients who had serious heart problems, just standing in this building gave him a new appreciation of the fragility of life. To fight a disease that insists on winning is scary.

"I don't want your name on it either." David grabbed her hand, taking in everything around him as they walked slowly to the elevator. Jillian seemed completely unmoved by the surroundings. She had spent enough time here to become unaffected.

Then he saw it—a large poster with the images of Jillian, in a blue sweater with a blue-and-white scarf on her head, alongside Tara, head also scarved, wearing a pink shirt embellished with the word *Supporter*. Tara's face was full, and Jillian's was painfully thin. Her cheekbones were too prominent. Both had huge grins and were giving the thumbs up sign. What was missing in Jillian's eyes, that Tara's had, was a sparkle.

He moved slowly toward the image. Intellectually he knew she'd had cancer. Tara had shown him a few pictures, but none were like this one. Here she was in treatment. Staring at the woman he loved, looking like this, tore at his heart.

He blinked a few times. At about the time she was going through this he had been recovering from his skiing accident. He had been feeling sorry for himself while she had literally been fighting for her life.

"That was taken on the last day of chemo. I think within minutes of that photo I was upchucking." With a faraway look, she continued. "Tara was usually the one who came with me. That day we went back to my house. Barb and my dad were there. There were balloons and a cake to celebrate. Well the cake was for them. I had chicken broth, but it was in a fancy bowl that Kyle and Emily had bought."

Up until that point, David had been holding her hand. He let go to pull Jillian close to him. He kissed her temple and closed his eyes to lean his forehead against the side of her head. He needed a moment to compose himself after seeing this picture.

"But it's all good. Look at me now," she said brightly. "I'm still here. I'm not letting it beat me." She was right.

Silently, they walked to the bank of elevators to ride to Dr. Brody's fourth-floor office. Outside the door, there was another picture of Jillian, not as big as the one in the lobby. The caption was *Race for the Cure*. She was still thin and with other pink-shirted, grinning women. What struck him were the wisps of hair that barely stuck out from the ball cap on her head. He'd never seen her with short hair. It had always been long, past her shoulders like it was now.

"I walk every year. The last walk was the weekend before my accident. Do you think you might walk it with me next year?"

Even with his limp, he knew he would to show support of everything she'd dealt with.

Inside the pink waiting room were more pictures of various patients. Jillian went to the reception desk and gave her name. She and the receptionist chatted like old friends.

When she sat down, she seemed subdued.

"It will be all right." He held her hand.

"I know." She squeezed his hand, realizing that he, too, needed comforting.

When her name was called, she stood up.

"Do you need me to go with you?" he asked.

"Not for this part," she said. "I'll have them come get you later."

She left through the door with the nurse. He watched the minute hand on the clock tick as he couldn't focus on the TV or any magazine articles. Waiting was the hardest thing in the world to do.

****

Jillian wished she could have captured a picture of David's face when he joined her in Dr. Brody's office. He was the one who had wanted to come with her. But now, not only was he tense, but lines of worry were etched deeply into his face.

From the look on Dr. Brody's face, she knew the results before he opened his mouth. She put her hands over her mouth, and any anxiety she was experiencing left her body. David breathed a huge sigh of relief. She listened as her oncologist reminded her it was something they would need to continue to watch, but the fact that she had hit this major milestone was huge. Really huge.

She and David held hands as they left the office. By the time they were outside the cancer center, Jillian was elated. She immediately called Tara, who screamed with excitement, and then her dad, who was happy.

Walking toward his car, David asked, "Can we stop by my place? I need to pick up some clothes."

"Sure," Jillian responded.

At his car, he kissed her deeply.

"How about we go out to celebrate tonight?" she asked when he started the car, "I'd like Tara and Peter to come along, too. I mean, they've been with me every step of the way."

"Whatever you want." He pulled onto the road toward his townhouse.

"It is." She smiled, knowing this just had to be a perfect day.

Pulling into his driveway, Jillian noticed a moving van a few driveways down, and wondered if, by chance, it was Cathy.

Once inside the house, she looked at the lake through the window in his back door. Maybe she should call upstairs and tell him to bring more over. He was spending more and more time at her place.

When the doorbell rang, she thought nothing of

answering it. Surprise! She was face-to-face with Cathy.

"Can I help you?" Jillian bit back the sarcasm that just begged to ooze out.

"Is David here?" Cathy asked, nonchalantly. "I was hoping he could come down and look at something for me."

"What do you need him to look at?" Jillian asked.

"It's none of your business. I need to see David."

"He's busy at the moment, and then we're out of here. And no, he's not coming down to see you." Jillian started to close the door. She was not about to let this hateful person ruin her day.

Cathy's hand flew out to stop the door from closing. "Now listen here. You may think you're back with David, but believe me, it is only temporary. You're nothing but a pretty face. You don't have what it takes, intellectually, to keep him. I do."

Jillian crossed her arms. "You know what Cathy? *You* listen to me. I'll share a little secret with you. I just heard the best news today. I kicked cancer, and that's even more deadly than you. I'm not going to let your jealousy and hatefulness ruin my day. You will not be coming between David and me anymore. So, goodbye." Jillian literally slammed the door in Cathy's face.

"Wow, remind me not mess with you." David was standing at the top of the stairs.

"I'm tired of her, and I'm not putting up with this anymore," Jillian said.

"That was a pretty strong hint to her." David descended the stairs. "I do love you."

"I know." She smiled as she bolted the front door. "Now, let's go home."

Chapter 32

When they turned onto her street, Jillian knew something was up. There were several familiar cars in front of her house. Getting closer, she saw the pink banner across her front porch reading *Congratulations*. Pink and white balloons lined the railing.

David shrugged his shoulders, but from the Cheshire grin on his handsome face, she knew he'd had a hand in this. "I think we're supposed to go in through the front door," he said.

"You think?"

His deep ice blue eyes were sparkling—so different from earlier today when they'd been so worried.

As they walked up the front steps, the door flew open. Tara ran out and practically tackled her to the ground with her exuberant hug. Tears of happiness filled her eyes, and Jillian's had to follow suit. Emily and Kyle, along with Peter, joined in the hug.

With camera in hand, Barb came onto the porch to take a picture of the group hug with Jillian buried somewhere in the middle.

David stood off to the side taking it all in, just like when they were younger.

"David, get your ass over here," Tara exclaimed.

"Yes, come join us," Jillian said.

Hesitantly, he encircled the group with his arms.

Carol, Jillian's dad, and others streamed onto the

porch,

"Come inside where it's warmer," her dad said.

Lynda and Eric were standing in the family room when they walked inside. Everyone talked at once. There had to be more than a hundred pink and white balloons everywhere. Lynda said, "We had the Party Store bring the helium tank here, and we started blowing up the balloons when you left this morning."

"And if the news wasn't good?"

"Well, you could have popped them in frustration," Tara said.

"Speaking of popping…" Peter shook a bottle of champagne to ensure the cork would go flying.

Jillian looked at the all the bottles.

"David bought them the other day and left them with Peter," Tara said reaching over Jillian's shoulder to accept a glass from David.

"Here's to my beautiful daughter who never gave up fighting," her dad toasted.

"Here's to *five years*," Lynda said.

"No, here's to ta-tas that need mindfulness." Tara lifted her glass.

"Thanks, and here's to everyone who supported me each step of the way." Jillian sniffled, trying her darnedest not to cry.

David put his arm around her and kissed the side of her head. His warm eyes let her know everything was okay and that he was here for her.

"Aunt Jillian, we have cake, too," Emily said. "Come see."

Following the group into the dining room, Jillian saw the table loaded with foods ranging from vegetables, to dip, to mini-sandwiches. A sheet cake was at the end of the table. Coming around, she saw the cake was in the shape of two boobs, discreetly iced with the image of a lacy pink bra.

"The woman at the bakery didn't want to do it at first. But after much convincing, she finally relented," Tara said, laughing. "Gawd, talk about being uptight."

Of course, Tara would think of something like this and not see anything wrong.

David magically appeared at her side. "Uh, did you still want to go out to dinner?"

"No, I guess not," Jillian said.

"Good. I know I couldn't think of a good exit line to get us out of here." He began loading sandwiches on a plate.

Looking around, she saw everyone filling plates and talking. It felt good to finally have that dark cloud lifted.

****

Tara and Jillian were in the kitchen cleaning up the last of the food and plates now that everyone had left.

Kyle and Emily had tossed a coin to see who would get the privilege of driving home to finish up their homework. David found it amusing when Jillian seemed nervous about them driving alone after having a single sip of champagne several hours earlier. He'd heard about helicopter moms but knew she just cared about them.

David sat in the keeping room, off the kitchen, where a small fire was burning. They discussed the possibility of another colder-than-average winter.

"Does that wreak havoc on your hip?" Peter asked.

"Yeah, I'm probably going to need a hip replacement before I'm fifty."

"Getting old sucks, doesn't it?" Tara came in from the kitchen and gave David a pointed look.

Jillian's back was to them, and she didn't see Tara mouthing words and pointing at her.

David shook his head and was about to mime "not now" when Jillian turned back around. She came to sit on the love seat next to him.

He broke eye contact with Tara. Instead his gaze never wavered from the woman he'd always loved. Jillian was as gorgeous today as she had been twenty years ago. In fact, he found her to be more beautiful than ever.

Earlier, when the party was in full swing, Kyle had set up a computer with a slideshow of Jillian's photos when she was battling cancer. David had watched the images flip from one to another for about ten minutes amazed how in each, she displayed a fighting spirit.

Her father joined him. "You know, there were worse times." He chuckled about her vanity. "Jillian wouldn't allow any photos when she was really sick."

Tara cleared her throat now, and David knew he had to take action before she blurted out his surprise, just to spite him.

He stood stiffly. "I'll be right back."

David returned and Tara was discussing their upcoming Christmas party. "I invited Eric and Lynda. I mean, hell, they just live right around the corner," Tara said in her throaty inflection.

David sat next to Jillian, holding two envelopes in this hand. "I don't mean to interrupt, but I have a little something to give you—to celebrate today's news."

He gave one envelope to Jillian. She took it hesitantly. "You don't need to give me anything." She stared at him.

"Yes. He does," Tara and Peter said in unison.

Jillian looked at the two of them suspiciously. She slowly opened the envelope. Inside were two sheets of paper. Her eyes scanned the pages. "I don't understand." It was at that moment realization hit her. "Omigawd, these are tickets to Paris…in June. We're going to Paris?"

"Yes, we are." he said smiling.

Peter handed the other envelope from David to Tara who greedily opened it. She exclaimed, "Omigawd, David, you bought us tickets, too?"

"No. I bought ours." Peter's eyes rolled and an eyebrow lifted.

"We're going, too?" Tara cried out.

Jillian looked from Tara to David, and then back to the tickets.

He knew the second she finally saw the most important thing on the ticket—the name.

Her hand flew to cover her mouth, and her eyes met his again. "This says, Jillian Rainer," she whispered.

He nodded his head. Tara, who had been keeping the box, had set it on the counter next to David earlier when they were cleaning the kitchen. He reached in his jacket pocket now. "Jillian, will you marry me?" He slipped Nana's wedding ring, reset with emeralds around the diamond, on her finger.

"Of course. I never thought you were going to ask." She hugged and kissed him.

"So, no more worrying about shacking up, huh?" Tara asked. "Is he finally going to be allowed to move some clothes over permanently?

David felt himself blushing. He'd mentioned this to Tara a few weeks ago when they were driving to her dad's to talk about Nana's ring.

"Some? I think all. Especially now that Glasses has taken up residence two doors down from him."

Jillian was still looking at the ring. "What if we get married next month…have a Christmas wedding?"

"If that's what you want, then let's do it." He grinned. He wasn't going to make the same mistake as before.

Jillian's eyes sparkled as she nodded.

"And we get to go with you two to Paris," Tara said with glee. She slapped her husband. "I can't believe you were in on this."

"Hey, you aren't the only one who has been talking and planning with David. We put our heads together that night at the pub. Imagine what wouldn't have been arranged if you women ever went to the bathroom by yourselves."

"All this sneaking around behind my back!" Jillian's eyes narrowed. "I never knew you were this good at surprises."

From the look on his future's wife face, David knew he had scored with this one.

Chapter 33

Jillian was snuggled into bed against David and glad they didn't need to get up to head to work. He was still asleep. She gazed at her hand amazed that he, or maybe it was Tara, remembered her talking about Nana's ring. Jillian had actually assumed it was buried with her.

Later this morning they, along with Peter, Kyle, and Eric, were heading to his place to move the things he was keeping. She had cleared her spring and summer clothes out of her closet to give him space for his clothes. They would move the dresser in from the other room so he would have a place to put his stuff.

She couldn't believe this was happening. Tomorrow she, Tara, Emily, and Barb were going shopping for a simple wedding dress. Then it was on to the McClure Country Club, where her dad, Tara, and Peter belonged, to arrange for the reception dinner.

She ran her recently uncasted hand along David's hard chest and rock-hard abs—a nice by-product of his almost-daily swims.

"You know what that does to me?" David asked sleepily.

She propped her head up on her hand, "What?" she innocently replied. She ran her hand lower to touch more of her favorite body parts.

He reached over and cupped her breast.

"Does it bother you that they're fake?" she said.

"No. It means you're still here with me." He pulled her on top of him to make love.

Each time he was inside her, she felt complete. Making love with David was never boring. He seemed to know exactly what to do to bring her to new heights.

When they were done, she laid on top of him. After a few minutes she slid off him. "Sorry to be crushing you."

He pulled her so close their bodies were practically one. "You can never crush me. You weigh close to nothing." His hand brushed along the lower part of her back, sending tingles up her spine.

"What time are the guys coming over?" Jillian burrowed back down under the covers.

"I told them to meet us here at 9:30 so we can get the rental van." He rolled to face her. "Are you sure you're okay with me moving in?"

"In less than a month, we'll be married. I'm sure it's okay." She kissed his nose. She knew they had to get up and shower, but right now this was heaven.

****

Actually there were not a lot of things he was moving into Jillian's. In talking to the real estate agent, David had decided to leave most of the furniture in his place and include it as part of the deal. He did, however, want to take the desk and bookshelf from his office. He would set it up in the room off that kitchen that faced the side of the house. Jillian's treadmill and exercise ball, currently residing in that room, would have no problem relocating elsewhere in the large Victorian she had assured him.

They were loading the television and the last of the

pictures when Eric saw Cathy approaching. "Great. Look who's here," he grumbled.

"Who's that?" Peter asked setting his end of the TV down.

"That's Cathy." David was holding the box of cords for all the electronics.

"What's going on here?" Cathy asked. "Oh...hi Eric.

Eric stared at her. "Hey Cathy,"

She immediately introduced herself to Peter, "I don't think I've met you before."

"Peter is Tara's husband," David said. "You remember Tara, Jillian's best friend."

"Oh," Cathy said, clearly giving Peter the once over. "So what *is* going on here?" she asked again.

Eric answered, "David and Jillian are getting married."

"What!" Cathy spun around to look at David.

Eric was a little surprised that more than her head spun the hundred-and-eighty degrees.

"That's right. Selling the place," David said. "Got any friends who might be interested? Now if you'll excuse us, Cathy, we're busy here."

Eric elbowed Peter and stage-whispered, "That's a good one...Cathy and friends."

She trailed after David as he walked back to the front door.

Kyle was coming out with a box. "Aunt Jillian's almost done inside." He passed by, ignoring Cathy.

Cathy grabbed at the back of David's shirt.

He spun around to glare at her. "Don't you ever touch me again," he said.

"Have you lost your mind?" Cathy hissed. "You've

been back together, what? A few months? How do you know she won't leave you again?"

"She's my soulmate and the person I've loved all these years. It doesn't matter that we've only been back together a short time. All I know, is I can't live another day without her. I want her to be the last thing I hold before I go to sleep and the first thing I see when I wake up. Knowing she wants to also spend the rest of her life with me makes me the happiest man in the world."

"I can't believe you," Cathy whispered through clench teeth. "I could've given you that happiness if you gave me a chance."

"Fat chance." Jillian came up to David and kissed him on his cheek.

She looked sexy in her jeans and UK sweatshirt, her hair pulled into a ponytail. Of course the lace panties and bra she was sporting underneath—he'd watched her dress that morning—only added to the effect. Jillian carried an aura about her that made people want to be with her. Cathy didn't have that.

Jillian smiled at her fiancé. "I heard what you said. And I love you even more for saying it." With a fragment of a smile she looked at Cathy.

Eric took this opportunity to join them. "Hey Cathy. I think it's time for you to beat it. We're busy here."

Cathy swiveled on her heel so fast she practically lost her footing. She quickly walked away.

David could only wish this would be the last time he'd ever see her.

****

It was late on Thursday afternoon when David

emerged from his office, having just finished up his paperwork. The number of scheduled appointments during Christmas was fewer, but he knew activity in the ER would increase.

He was going to be off on Friday, and Saturday was the wedding. Jillian, Tara, and Barb had pulled it off. It was going to be a modest gathering, with close friends and family only.

When he'd announced his upcoming marriage a few weeks ago, the other cardiologists in the group were stunned. He'd explained it was a small affair, but it was agreed that they would go out tonight for "bachelor drinks."

Dan popped his head into David's office "Ready to leave?" he asked.

"Yep." David shut down his computer.

"Man, I still can't believe you two are back together."

Before David had a chance to respond, they heard Helen's voice booming from the front of the office. "If you don't leave, I will have to call security."

"I know he's back there," Cathy said. "I have an appointment. He and I talked about it last night."

"No, you didn't," Helen said loudly.

David and Dan walked up the hall and saw Helen picking up the phone.

Cathy shrieked. "I came to tell you I'm leaving, David."

"Leaving?" David asked, not quite understanding.

"I'm heading back to Atlanta where the people I worked with like me. I just wanted to come and say goodbye. You know I came up here to be with you. But then you hooked up with Jillian and completely dropped me."

"Uh, Cathy…we were never seeing each other," David answered.

Cathy rolled her eyes. "I just can't believe you treated me like this. I am done, and I'm leaving you. So…goodbye."

David responded flatly, "Goodbye." It was an effort to keep celebratory excitement from his voice.

When Cathy stormed out the door, Helen added, "Don't let the door hit you on the ass."

Dan looked at David. "What was that all about?"

"I have no idea. I wonder if, in her delusional way, she thinks she just broke up with me."

Helen interrupted, "I hate to break it to both of you, but I know, from a very reliable source, she was *asked* to seek employment elsewhere."

"Really?" Dan said.

David knew Helen's daughter worked as an anesthesiologist. That was probably her source. Well, at least Cathy was gone.

"Now, are we going out for those drinks?" Dan asked.

"Hell, yes. We'll have an extra to help heal my broken heart."

Chapter 34

The weatherman had predicted snow, but none had fallen yet when the Rolls Jillian's father had rented pulled in front of the church. Jillian looked at the man who was going to walk her down the aisle again. "I love you, Dad," she said.

"I love you, too. Now let's get going so you can do what you should have done in the first place. Not that I minded Brian, but you didn't look radiant, like you do now, on that wedding day.

She, Tara, and her dad got out of the car and walked quickly into the church. Barb ushered them into a side room before leaving to take her seat.

Jillian put her cream-colored cape on the side chair. She had fallen in love with it on their shopping trip. She looked in the mirror at her dress one more time. The beaded bodice of the cream, straight-skirted satin dress complimented the off-the-shoulder fur-trimmed neckline. She wore no veil, but had long, elbow-length gloves.

Tara beamed at her. Just as she was about to say something there was a knock.

"Who is it?" Jillian's dad asked.

"Eric. I came to see how you're doing. The groom is eager to get this going." He peered into the room. "You look beautiful, Jillian."

Tara cleared her throat, "Get out of here. You just

go tell your best friend that he'd better be good to her, or he'll have me to contend with."

Eric was chuckling as he left the room.

Soon, they could hear the organ music playing. From where they were standing, Jillian saw David and Eric take their places at the front of the church. Tara handed her the bouquet of white roses before she proceeded to sway her hips down the aisle. Good ol' Tara. She needed a little attention, too.

Jillian scanned the small group of assembled people. She wanted this to be a serene and joyous occasion.

"It's time, sugar," her father said softly for only her to hear. She stood there. Her legs wouldn't move. "Let's go. I think someone is waiting for you."

She and David made eye contact, and she floated the rest of the way down the aisle. There were no other faces around her. All her attention was on David. He was so handsome and regal standing there waiting for her.

Her heart was beating so hard that she wondered if everyone could hear it. She gulped in air and kept walking. When her father lifted her hand from his to David's, she was shaking with anticipation. She glanced up at his calming smile.

Halfway through the ceremony, David whispered to her, "I'm the luckiest man in the world."

She pinched his hand. "I just hope this is real, and not a dream."

He grinned at her.

At the end, when the priest pronounced them husband and wife, she did not wait for the line that the husband could kiss the bride. She exuberantly threw her arms around him and practically knocked him to the ground.

There were peals of laughter throughout the church when the priest announced, "The script says the groom can kiss the bride, not the bride can attack the groom."

After the ceremony they walked up the aisle to the room where her cape had been left. David pinned her against the wall and kissed her deeply before trailing kisses along the neckline of her dress. "You have made me the happiness man on this earth."

He placed the cape over her shoulders and together they left the room as Dr. and Mrs. Rainer.

Exiting the church's portal, they saw snow had started to fall. Jillian looked up at the sky and mouthed the words, "Thank you, Nana."

She was finally joined with the love of her life.

A word about the author…

Before moving to Northern Kentucky, Andrea lived in Atlanta, Georgia, for twenty years. While in Atlanta and traveling for her corporate sector career, she became inspired to write women's fiction. There were too many stories told amongst friends and strangers on planes to not put them on paper. Since she travels with 'Karma,' she is often stuck in airports and passes her times eavesdropping on conversations to use them for stories.

She is married and has two teenage children who keep her busy with their activities.

Thank you for purchasing
this publication of The Wild Rose Press, Inc.

If you enjoyed the story, we would appreciate your
letting others know by leaving a review.

For other wonderful stories,
please visit our on-line bookstore at
www.thewildrosepress.com.

For questions or more information
contact us at
info@thewildrosepress.com.

The Wild Rose Press, Inc.
www.thewildrosepress.com

Stay current with The Wild Rose Press, Inc.

Like us on Facebook

https://www.facebook.com/TheWildRosePress

And Follow us on Twitter
https://twitter.com/WildRosePress

CPSIA information can be obtained
at www.ICGtesting.com
Printed in the USA
LVHW021344050222
710362LV00008B/497